KILLIAN'S SECRET

ALICIA MONTGOMERY

Killian's Secret

Book 1 of the Lone Wolf Defenders
By

Alicia Montgomery

ALSO BY ALICIA MONTGOMERY

The True Mates Series

Fated Mates

Blood Moon

Romancing the Alpha

Witch's Mate

Taming the Beast

Tempted by the Wolf

Copyright © 2017 Alicia Montgomery
Cover design by Melody Simmons
Edited by LaVerne Clark at Free Bird Editing

All rights reserved.

To my Great Grandmother.

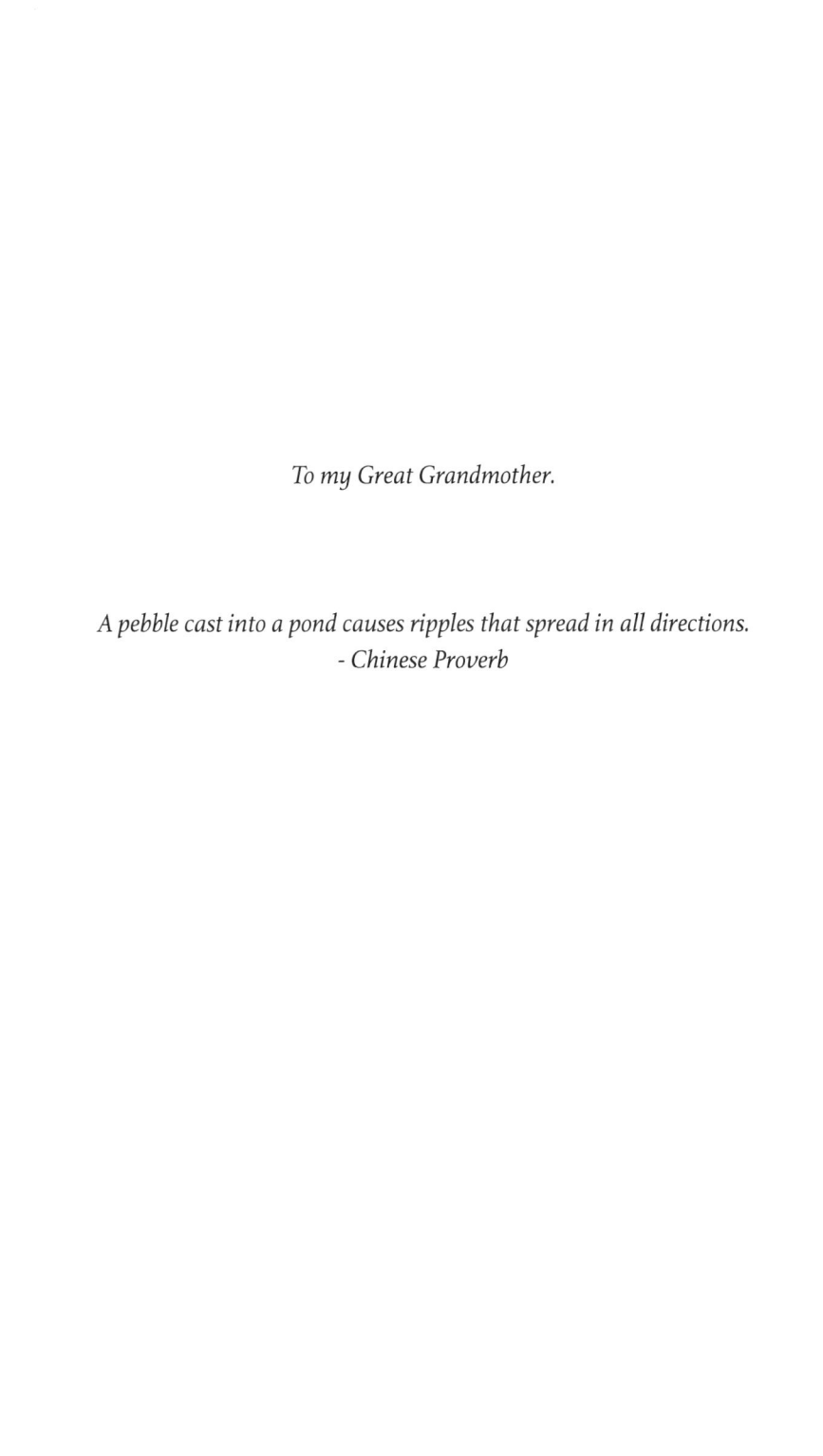

A pebble cast into a pond causes ripples that spread in all directions.
- Chinese Proverb

PROLOGUE

4 Months Ago...

The tapestry hanging on the wall looked like any ordinary rug to Killian's eyes. Smaller than he'd expected, and like something in those big box home improvement stores. The designs on the carpet were geometrical and archaic—a large diamond in the middle woven with brown, black, and red threads, surrounded by smaller diamonds in similar colors. The border followed the same color scheme but had a floral pattern (or what looked like flowers to his untrained eyes). Frankly, Killian didn't know what the fuss was about. But the rug was apparently important enough to warrant a display room in the Portland Museum of Art and for the Mornavian government to hire him to steal it.

This was his first job alone. Usually, he worked with his mentor and adoptive father, Archie Leacham, and his siblings, doing whatever jobs the older man had found for them. Corporate espionage, surveillance, protection and security, and major heists now and then—there was no job too big for their merry little family of professional thieves, hackers, and mercenaries. As long as no one got hurt or killed, they did it. It was what they were trained to do and what they were good at.

However, wanting to expand his skills as a master thief and spread his wings, Killian had decided he would try to do this one without them; after all, the current Mornavian president, Bogdan Martinov, had met him personally and pleaded his case. Archie had been quite proud he'd decided to strike out on his own, and offered advice whenever he needed it. Quinn was only too happy to take off and go backpacking in Europe, but not before helping him get set up with a few tech things, mainly his cover and background. Connor...well, he wasn't sure when he'd use his last brother's *unique* set of skills, but Killian knew that if he needed someone's face bashed in or leg broken, he could count on him. And his sister, Meredith? Well—

"It's lovely, isn't it?" came a voice from behind, interrupting his thoughts.

The hairs on his arms rose, the prickling sensation startling his inner wolf. As a Lycan shifter, the wolf was part of him. He was grateful for the speedy healing and enhanced senses, but the wolf didn't always make its presence obvious. Now the animal perked up, something it rarely did. Only when it was warning him of something important. Or of danger. He'd learned to trust it over the years.

Killian turned around, and for a moment he thought he had imagined the voice, as there was no one behind him. But, looking down, he saw a petite woman staring up at him in wonder, her large, violet eyes widening. He swallowed a gulp as his eyes traced over the rest of her features. Her gorgeous face with high cheekbones and milky white skin. Silvery hair was pinned up on top of her head, though a few tendrils softened her face and brushed against her delicate collarbones.

Her pink lips parted, and his keen senses picked up the slightest gasp. And her perfume? Cinnamon, sugar, and freshly-baked pastry. Such an unusual choice for a woman, one he'd never smelled before.

"It certainly is..." He grasped for words, losing his composure for a split second. "Interesting."

She laughed, her voice tinkling like little silver bells. "I know it can be a bit underwhelming, especially with all the promotion and press it's been getting. But I assure you, there's more to the *Gastlava Tapestry* than meets the eye." Her lovely face brightened, her cheeks coloring with excitement.

"Oh really?"

"Well, I'm sure you've heard about it? And the controversy behind it?"

Of course he had. That was why he was here, and why he was going to steal the rug. But something about the woman, the eagerness in her eyes, made him want to make sure she stayed right where she was standing. "No, I haven't. Do tell."

"Well," she began, pursing her lips. "The *Gastlava Tapestry* is one of the oldest known woven works in existence. It was excavated in 1941 in what is now the modern Mornavia in the Balkan mountains," she explained. "The tapestry itself was dated back to the fifth century BC. It's quite unique, not just for its age, but also the unusual pattern of the border. Back then, weavers weren't very skilled, but if you look at rugs from around the same time, few of them had such intricate designs or bold colors. The weaver must have been very talented or used a special loom that was—" She flushed again, and this time it wasn't with excitement. "Sorry, I tend to babble on about this."

"It's alright," he replied. "Please, go on."

"I won't bore you with the details, but I'm sure you'd like to hear about the controversy." She turned to the rug. "As you've probably heard, Mornavia has been in a state of civil war for the past fifteen years, thanks to Milos Fedosiovic, the former dictator. Two years ago, a bloodless revolution overthrew Fedosiovic, when the people of Mornavia took to the streets. He fled the country, along with, according to rumors, many of the priceless artworks and antiques from the Mornavia National Museum."

Killian stared at her, watching the shifts in her expression as she told the story and the way the colors in her eyes changed under the lights. He wasn't disinterested, but he already knew the story. No one had realized the tapestry was missing until it had resurfaced six months ago, in the hands of the notorious and flashy Portland-based hedge fund manager, Larry Bakersfield, who claimed it had been legally sold to him by the previous administration. The Mornavian government demanded the return of the piece, and even lobbied the US government, but to no avail. Bakersfield's net worth was bigger than Mornavia's GDP and he had powerful friends in Washington and everywhere else. He lawyered up, and refused to return the piece, despite the wave of bad publicity. He also hired a PR firm, who had apparently arranged this showing at the Portland Museum of Art, to show the world that Larry Bakersfield was a generous patron of the arts, not an egomaniacal bastard who would steal from a war-torn country. And tonight was the big gala, the unveiling of the exhibit centered around the *Gastlava Tapestry*.

"And so here we are," she concluded, and then looked back to Killian.

"You seem so knowledgeable, Ms...?"

"Rhoades. Luna Rhoades. Assistant Curator for the Portland Museum of Art."

Ah, a gallerina. Probably one of those artsy-fartsy types who went through four years of liberal arts school on daddy's dime and now has her dream job thanks to years of mummy's tea socials and charity galas. He should have known, looking at her expensive dress and jewelry.

"And you're okay with this, having this tapestry here, despite the negative press around it?" he challenged.

Luna's back stiffened. "Thanks to, uh, Mr. Bakersfield, we have the tapestry on display for an entire year, for everyone to enjoy."

Killian did not miss the hitch in her voice and the distaste in her eyes when she mentioned Bakersfield's name. "So you agree with him? And his way of doing things?"

Anger briefly flashed in her violet eyes and her fingers curled into fists at her sides. "My personal opinion on the matter is private, especially in this room. I represent the Portland Museum of Art, and we are grateful for Mr. Bakersfield's contribution."

Contribution. He bet it was a generous one, too. He opened his mouth to speak but was interrupted.

"Do I care for politics? Not at all. But at least here, people will actually get to see the tapestry, rather than it being locked away in some billionaire's private collection," she retorted.

"Ah, a true art lover," Killian replied.

Her slim shoulders sagged. "Or a realist." She lowered her voice. "I know that Mornavia doesn't stand a chance of getting the rug back, but at least here..." She shrugged and shook her head. "I'm sorry, I didn't catch your name, Mr...?"

"Jones. Killian Jones," he said smoothly, offering her his hand. When her delicate fingers touched his, he felt the crackle of electricity. Whether she felt it too, he wasn't sure, but the expression on her face told him she felt *something*.

"Oh," she gasped. "You're the representative from Grover Real Estate Holdings?"

Killian nodded confidently. Quinn was good at what he did, and he'd set up a fake company and made him a top executive, complete with bio and social media accounts. On the surface, he really was Killian Jones, VP for Operations of Grover Real Estate Holdings. Getting into the gala had been a snap, especially when he hinted that his company was looking to make a sizable donation.

"I spoke with your assistant," Luna recalled. "I'm sorry we initially overlooked your company this year, but I'm glad the invitation made its way to you."

"I'm glad, too," he said meaningfully, and she blushed. "So, Ms. Rhoades, you're the assistant curator. Do you have any favorite exhibits or pieces?"

The question made her eyes light up again, and the mood around them relaxed. "I can't possibly answer that! That would be like asking me who my favorite child is! Not that I have any. Children, that is," she added quickly.

"Why don't you show me around?" he said, offering his arm. "And then I'll try to guess which ones are your favorites. I promise I won't tell."

Luna eyed him suspiciously, but he noticed the smile tugging at the sides of her mouth. He cocked his head provocatively, and after a heartbeat, she took his arm. "Alright then, Mr. Jones. Let's start with the Impressionists..."

1

Present Day...

Killian rubbed the spot between his eyebrows and prayed to any God listening to make his headache go away. He looked around the office reception area at the piles of folders scattered all over the place, the dirty coffee cups on various surfaces, and the general mess. Letting out a deep sigh, Killian stepped over the many unopened boxes and made his way to the door at the end of the hallway. The other two offices next to his were still dark which meant he was the first one in today. Not that the three employees (namely himself and his two brothers, Connor and Quinn) of Lone Wolf Security kept regular hours, but he was always the first one in. He had an appointment at eleven this morning, so he wanted some time to himself before his brothers arrived.

Flipping on the switch, he glanced around his office. Apart from the fine layer of dust that had settled in the days he'd been away, everything else was relatively clean and tidy. Their boss,

Sebastian Creed, sent them to South America to deal with local gangsters terrorizing factory workers. Their client, the owner of said factory, was having problems with thugs who were intimidating the workers, stopping them from coming to work unless the owner paid them to go away. Needless to say, Lone Wolf Security had dealt with them, but it had taken longer than they'd expected. They were supposed to have come back forty-eight hours ago, but the operation had gone tits up. Thankfully, he and his brothers were professionals, and they were able to get out of trouble, if a little later than expected. They arrived back in New York late last night, and while it would have been reasonable to sleep in—he couldn't. Not when he'd rescheduled this meeting three times already. He wasn't going to do it a fourth time.

Killian sat at his desk and booted up his computer. Once he'd gone through his emails, he sorted the other mundane administrative tasks. By the time he was done, he wished he was back in that mud hut in South America, surrounded by goons with semi-automatic weapons.

He let out a loud sigh. They needed help and they needed it now. An admin assistant would make a difference and get the office in order.

Glancing at the clock, he saw it was nearly eleven. The front door opened and he stood up and stretched, ready to conduct this interview. However, the bundle of energy who rushed into his office was not the interviewee.

"Kiiillllian!" Meredith, his adopted sister, greeted as she slammed the door behind her. The blonde woman tossed her winter coat on the couch in the corner and then plopped herself on the chair in front of his desk. She set cardboard coffee holder on his desk and handed him one of the cups. "When did you get back?"

He accepted the cup with a grateful nod. "Last night."

"Where did Creed send you this time?" she asked. "And what did you have to deal with?"

"South America. Thugs with AK-47s. You know."

"The usual," she finished with a smile. "What time did you get in this morning? And where are Connor and Quinn?"

"Around eight. Probably still sleeping in."

"And you are here because…"

"Interview for the new admin assistant," he said, taking a sip from the coffee cup.

Meredith pouted. "You're replacing me?"

"You know—barging in here and messing around with our files doesn't make you our official admin assistant."

"You didn't complain when I volunteered at first. And I do such a good job!"

Killian laughed and then choked on his coffee, the liquid coming out of his nose down his shirt.

"Christ!" he cursed and grabbed some napkins to clean himself up.

"Oh ha, ha," Meredith said. "Serves you right."

He took a deep breath. "If you do such a good job, then what's with all the boxes and shit in the lobby?"

"Hey, you wanted an assistant, not a cleaning lady," she retorted. "An admin usually does filing and appointments, right?"

"Yeah, but they file things alphabetically," he said, glancing at the file cabinet behind him.

"I did file alphabetically."

"Yeah, you put the client report files in folders like; 'Assface', 'Bastard' , and 'Cunt' ," he pointed out.

"That is alphabetical, Killian," she retorted. "Besides, it's not a reflection on your clients—just the things you had to deal with based on what I read in your reports. So, what am I supposed to do now? I don't have a job, my husband is working his ass off, and we have a baby on the way."

"Right," he replied wryly. "Still, we both know that you don't need the job. Didn't you just buy half of a loft in Tribeca?" Besides their generous shares from jobs over the years, Archie Leacham left his adopted children his entire estate when he died. He and his siblings had enough money in this lifetime and the next.

"Yeah, but I like coming here," she sulked, standing up and walking over to him. "And I'm bored! I'm pretty much alone at home. Daric and Jade have limited me to visiting the lab only three times a week. They said they're not sure if the baby should be exposed to all the experiments there, but I think it's because I'm always distracting them."

"Why would they think that?" he asked sarcastically, which earned him a dirty look. "Look, if you like coming here, you know you're always welcome to hang out. But we need someone who can get things in shape, at least help us unpack and file things, answer emails and such." The sound of the door buzzer interrupted him. "Speaking of which…"

"I'll get him!" Meredith said,. "I wanna be the first to size up the competition."

Before he could say anything, she was out of her chair, darting out to the reception area. He heard the sound of the front door opening and excited voices. One minute later, his sister came back.

"Right this way," Meredith said cheerfully, stepping aside to let the other person behind her in. "I didn't know you were interviewing a girl," she exclaimed. "Finally—another female! It won't be such a sausage fest around here. Killian, this is Guinevere King. I love that name, don't you?"

Killian's eyes narrowed as he observed Guinevere King. For some reason, she looked familiar, but he couldn't quite put his finger on where he'd seen her before. He would have remembered for sure. She was cute he supposed; almost exotic with her soft brown eyes that turned up slightly at the corner, a pert nose with a sprinkling of freckles, and prominent cheeks on a softly rounded face. Her long, brown hair was pulled back into a ponytail. The skirt suit she wore looked new, but was definitely off the rack as it seemed a tad short for her frame and didn't fit her curves quite right. He had read her résumé of course, and frankly he was so desperate, he would have offered her the job the moment she walked in the door. Guinevere King had the right qualifications after all. The only qualification that mattered. Although a human, she knew all about Lycans.

"Ms. King," Killian greeted and offered his hand.

"Mr...ugh..." Guinevere's brows knitted. "Sorry," she mumbled.

"Just call me Killian." He and his siblings weren't any regular Lycans. They were Lone Wolves and had no clan which also meant they carried no last name. As a consequence, he'd had his share of fake surnames over the years.

"Then please, call me Evie."

"Such an unusual name," he observed. "Hope you weren't teased a lot when you were a kid?"

She gave a nervous laugh. "You should talk to my brother, Arthur."

He gave her a wry smile. "All right, Evie, let's start." He motioned to the chair, and she sat down, smoothing her skirt and crossing her legs at the ankles. He waited for Meredith to leave, but instead, she sat down on the chair beside Evie and shot him an impatient look.

Killian sighed and shrugged. "Thank you for coming in," he said to the newcomer. "I'm sorry I had to keep canceling our past appointments."

"No worries," she said. "I understand you must be very busy since you have a new business and all."

"Right." He took the folder with her résumé and peered down at it. "Well, I suppose given your background, you know all about us?"

She nodded. "Cady Vrost reached out to me," she said, mentioning the name of the New York Clan's Human Liaison. Although Killian, Connor, and Quinn were still technically Lone Wolves, they had permission from the Alpha to stay and set up shop in the city, mostly thanks to Meredith who had pledged to them. "You need an administrative assistant who could come in a few hours a week. Specifically, she said your business was Lycan-related, so it would have to be someone who knew about Lycans."

"Sebastian Creed, CEO of Creed Security, asked us to head an offshoot of his company. One that he could tap to deal with special ops," Killian explained. "My brothers and I are Lycans, and since we do jobs by ourselves, we can use our abilities without worrying about human team members finding out about our secret. Initially, we just want someone who can help us unpack the office, do some computer work, and of course, file our reports to Creed. That person has to know about Lycans since our reports have details that pertain to shifting and our abilities."

"Ah, I see," Evie nodded.

"But, you're human? Originally from Kansas City?"

"Yes, that's right. My mother is a Lycan and my father is human, though they divorced a while back. I'm properly registered with the Kansas City clan of course, and I'm pledged to obey all Lycan laws."

His eyes darted over her résumé again. "So, you've got some experience working in an office?"

"Yes," she stated. "I've been working at my father's furniture store since I was fourteen. I did the general filing and some light bookkeeping, filling in for his secretary when she was sick or on vacation. I worked full-time there for a year too when I was trying to figure out what I wanted to do."

"And why did you move to New York City?"

"I wanted to become a Broadway actress. I mean, I am an actress," she replied, sitting up straight in her chair.

"*Oooh*," Meredith interjected. "Are you any good? Have I seen you in anything?"

"Er, probably not," she replied in an embarrassed voice. "I did a lot of regional theater back in Kansas, but I'm not in anything right now. I'm mostly doing auditions and casting calls, so my schedule's pretty open," Evie explained. "And, if I do get into a show, call time at the theater isn't until four o'clock for evening shows, and I promise I'll—"

"You're hired," Killian stated. "I'm sure we can work around your schedule, as long as you get the work done. We don't entertain walk-ins or have meetings here, so there's no need for a full-time receptionist."

Evie's eyes widened. "Really? Oh my God! Thank you," she squealed. "I mean—this is pretty awesome."

"It's just unpacking and filing," he reminded her. "Nothing glamorous, and it's only twenty hours a week."

"No, it's great. It means I don't have to pick up as many shifts at the diner," she said with a sigh of relief.

"Can you start tomorrow?"

"Of course!"

"Great." Killian stood up and she followed suit. He walked over to her and held out his hand. "Welcome to Lone Wolf Security, Evie King."

She grabbed his hand and shook it enthusiastically. "Thank you, Boss. You won't regret it, I promise."

"I'm sure I won't," Killian nodded. "Now, let's get you—" The door to his office slammed open, interrupting him before he could finish.

Connor's large frame filled the doorway as he stalked inside. His brother's face looked tired like he'd had another sleepless night, and the scar that ran down the right side of his face seemed deeper today. "Hey, Killian, what the—*You!*" Connor's eyes zeroed in on Evie, his face drawing into a scowl.

Killian could smell the fear and tension rolling off the human, and heard her heartbeat speed up like a jackhammer. "I...I didn't know...you..." She looked back at Killian. "*Oh my God,* I thought you looked familiar!"

"What's going on?" Killian felt another headache coming on. "Have we met before?"

"The night at Merlin's," Connor growled. "She hit me with her purse."

"It's because you were a stupid and obstinate ox," Evie accused, and then slapped her hand over her mouth. Her face fell. "I'm sorry. Sorry about this. I'm...I'll go now. Thank you for the interview."

Meredith's eyes were darting from Connor, to Evie's retreating form, and back to Killian. "Wait—what's going on here? How do you know Evie again?"

"She was that girl who caused trouble for us at that witch strip club," Connor snarled. "Everything was going fine with our op, and then she tried to get in, all liquored up, causing a scene, and I wouldn't let her through."

"As I recall," Meredith began. "It was Quinn going full Lycan in a room full of witches and warlocks that caused trouble for us."

"What the fuck was she doing there, anyway?" Connor growled. "A Lycan in a witch strip joint?"

"She's not a Lycan, moron," Meredith shot back.

"Then why does she—"

"Yo, what's up?" Quinn walked in casually. He was still wearing his winter coat and his laptop bag was slung casually over his shoulder. "Who's the cute skirt I saw running out of here? Connor, did she see your ugly mug and run the other direction?"

Connor let out a growl—a real one—and his eyes turned to steel.

"Don't you start, Quinn," Killian groaned. "Is she still out there?"

His brother shrugged. "Probably. Waiting on the elevator, maybe. You know that rickety old thing takes ages."

"Good." Before any of them could protest, he rushed out, hoping he wasn't too late. As he jogged towards the elevator, he saw Evie pacing in front of the door, muttering to herself and shaking her head.

"Shit...goddammit...f—Oh! Killian," she exclaimed as he drew nearer. "Look, I'm sorry, I didn't know. I mean, I don't remember much from that night, but I assure you I don't make a habit of hanging around male strip clubs. You see, my best friend—"

"Don't worry about it," he said, raising a hand to stop her. "What you do in your private life isn't any of my business. You've been vetted by both the New York Clan and Cady Vrost, so I'm sure you didn't have any nefarious reason for being there."

"No, I swear I didn't. Just a girls' night out gone wrong."

"Good." Now he vaguely recalled her. That night at Merlin's was a little bit foggy in his mind seeing as he'd been hit with some type of confusion potion when things went down. He did remember having to rescue Connor from a bunch of angry women at some point. His brother was never smooth with the ladies and it looked like Evie King had gotten under Connor's skin for some reason. "Now, I'll expect you here tomorrow then. We'll have to fill in forms and—"

"Wait—what?" Evie looked up at him, a soft gasp escaping her mouth. "You want me to come back?"

"Of course." There was no other alternative, after all.

"But what about...him?"

He frowned. "Connor?"

She nodded. "He doesn't seem to like me very much."

"He doesn't spend a lot of time at the office," Killian assured her. "Most of our ops are overseas. In fact, you won't see very much of any of us, I'm afraid. You'll have the freedom to come and go anytime you like to complete your twenty hours."

She didn't look convinced. Her lips were pursed and she was wringing her hands. He didn't want to scare her off, not when he was tired of looking for someone to fill in the position. He took her by the elbow. "Listen, Evie, I'll be honest with you. We don't have any other qualified candidates. There aren't a lot of Lycans or humans in the know who want to work with us. Quinn, Connor, and me, are Lone Wolves. Do you know what that means?"

She nodded nervously. "Sort of. I mean, I've heard about them—er—you. You don't have clans for some reason or another and you usually roam around."

"Yes, that's true. It also means our wolves are..." He didn't want to use the word damaged because although that was true in Connor's case, he didn't want to scare her. "Restless. We don't have an Alpha to follow—to ground us. It makes other wolves nervous."

"I see," she said, biting her lip.

"Connor won't hurt you. He would never hurt a woman. If you want, I can give you a heads-up if he's going to be in the office so you don't have to see him."

"No," she protested, grabbing his arm. "I mean, no problem," she quickly added with a nervous laugh.

"Great," he replied. "You'll accept the position, then?"

"Yes," she said in a high-pitched voice. "Thank you so much for this."

A soft ding indicated that the ancient elevator had finally arrived. Killian grabbed the handle of the gate and pulled it open for her. Evie stepped inside, buttoning up her coat to prepare herself for the winter chill outside. "I'll see you in the morning, Boss," she said as he shut her inside.

He gave her a final wave as the elevator descended and then Ms. Evie King was gone. There was nothing mysterious about her, yet he couldn't help but feel intrigued. Fresh-faced and innocent, she had a bright demeanor that didn't have a hint of cynicism. It reminded him of—

No. Can't think about that. The anger began to bubble up inside of him, but he quickly shut it down. Things weren't always what they seemed. An innocent-looking lamb could sometimes be a wolf in sheep's clothing.

Shaking his head to clear his thoughts, Killian walked back into the office. As usual, his siblings were squabbling about something or other. It almost made him smile. Meredith had left them some time ago when she had a disagreement with their father, and although it was sad that it took his death to bring them back together, he couldn't help but feel nostalgic. It was just like old times.

"All right, stop. *Stop*," Killian commanded and the three other Lycans immediately quieted down. "What are you arguing about now?"

"Connor being a dickhole to Evie," Meredith barked. "I like her. I want to keep her. Even though she is taking my job."

"She's not a pet, Mer," Quinn quipped.

"You know what I mean," she snapped. "I have this feeling that we need her. And she needs us."

"You were always the one taking in strays like you were some

Disney princess," Quinn moaned. Beside him, Connor looked conflicted but nodded in agreement.

"She's not some lost animal," Killian said, holding his hand up before any of them could interject. "Listen to me. Evie is the most qualified person to help us out here. I've hired her. She'll come in on a part-time basis and work around our schedule if she has to. Don't scare her away," he warned. "That means, no growling at her," he said to Connor. "No hitting on her," he looked at Quinn. "And no smothering her with your constant need to get into everyone's business."

"Me?" Meredith batted her eyelashes when Killian's gaze landed on her. "When do I do that?"

He rolled his eyes. "If I have to reconcile another expense report or deal with the landlord over the bathrooms again, I swear I'm going to murder all of you." The threat was met with silence which he accepted as their agreement. "Okay then, if you guys are ready," he motioned to Connor and Quinn. "We need to debrief with Sebastian. He said to call his office any time today."

"How about lunch first?" Meredith asked. "I'm hungry."

"You're always hungry," Quinn said. "I know you've always eaten like a pig, but that kid you're growing inside you eats like a sumo wrestler."

"Shut up. That's your niece or nephew you're talking about," Meredith gave him a punch on the arm. "And besides, it's a magical baby, remember? Not just because my husband's a warlock, but also my True Mate. That means we were meant to be together and this baby was conceived the first time we banged in the backseat of—"

"*Eww*, please, I don't wanna hear about your soul mate sex life," Quinn interrupted.

"None of us do," Connor gruffed.

Killian shook his head. "Meredith, go ahead and order a

couple of pizzas or something. I'll call Sebastian and make an appointment."

Killian locked the door behind him, relieved that the day was finally over. Meredith hung around until after lunch and then left to go back home. After their conference call with Sebastian, Connor and Quinn left the office. He stayed behind preparing for the next day and making sure he had all of Evie's forms printed out.

He'd always thought he'd be a master thief his entire life, skirting the law and taking on jobs that would be on the gray side of things. It was the death of his father and wanting to keep his little ragtag family together that made him accept Sebastian's offer to move to New York from Portland. Of course, had he known going legit required so much paperwork, he might have had second thoughts.

He breathed in the crisp winter air outside as he stepped out of the building. It was already dark outside despite the early hour and the temperatures had dropped significantly. As a Lycan, he didn't feel cold, but he wore a coat anyway to keep up appearances. They all did, as the human world was not ready to know about the existence of wolf shifters living under their very noses for the last couple hundred years.

Killian headed uptown towards his condo in Kips Bay on the east side of Manhattan. Although it was over thirty blocks away, he didn't mind the walk. Normally, he took a cab or the subway, but he wanted to be outside and let out some excess energy. His inner wolf did not like being cooped up inside the office all day.

His walk took him to the busy area of Union Square. It was out of his way, but he liked the vibe there. The square was bustling, filled with students from the nearby universities hanging out at the park despite the chilly temperatures (probably to escape their cramped dorm rooms) and shoppers doing some after-Christmas bargain hunting. He was standing in front of Union Square Park on Fourteenth Street and Broadway, getting ready to cross the street when the hairs on the back of his neck prickled and something in the corner of his eye caught his attention.

A flash of silvery hair.

He turned his head to the right, eyes scanning the throng of people as they crossed the street towards the east side of Broadway. He towered over most of the crowd so he quickly spotted a female figure with silvery blonde hair under a black beanie. *No. It couldn't be.* His inner wolf perked up all of a sudden, turning its head, trying to catch a familiar scent. It scratched at him, telling him to go after her. *And then what?* He asked the wolf. What would he do if it was her?

His keen eyes tracked the woman in a black coat as she hurriedly crossed the street. He was seeing things. Besides, as far as he could see, the woman had a short bob, the hair stopping a few inches above her shoulders. Mentally shaking his head, he purged his thoughts of her. It was all his imagination. Luna Rhoades was not halfway across the street from him. She was all the way across the country. And he hoped the cold-hearted, icy bitch would stay there.

2

Luna's blood roared in her ears and her stomach tightened as she crossed Broadway. Her knees were shaking so bad she thought she would collapse in the middle of the busy intersection. Miraculously, she continued walking towards Third Avenue. As she got to the little bus shelter, she braced herself on the wall; her breathing heavy, sending little puffs of clouds into the air.

The man she saw was definitely Killian Jones. Or whatever his real name was. She was crossing Lafayette Street when she spied the familiar tall figure in the navy-blue coat walking uptown. She followed him for a few blocks and told herself it was to make sure it wasn't him. But, when he suddenly walked to the other side of the street, she saw his profile—dark brows, aquiline nose, firm mouth, and a strong, square jaw that the shadow of a beard couldn't hide. If she had come any closer, she probably would have gotten a whiff of his fresh, morning rain-scented cologne. That was definitely Killian, and as soon as she confirmed it, she turned tail, crossing to the other side of the street from him.

The M03 bus arrived, heaving as scores of people spilled out.

She got on, and a nice-looking young man stood up and motioned to the seat he had been occupying. Nodding her thanks, she eased onto the seat grateful for the chance to get off her feet. Chasing Killian for five city blocks hadn't been easy, and as she was going to spend another couple of hours on her feet, sitting down for a few minutes would make a big difference.

As she watched the city go by, her exhausted brain filled with questions. What was Killian doing in New York? Did he know she was there? Was he after her? She thought putting an entire country between them would mean never seeing him again. After all, it was his fault she was in this situation in the first place. *Shit.*

She would have to avoid Union Square now just in case he hung out there. She didn't want to see him and most of all didn't want to feel that flutter in her heart when she realized he was right there in front of her, close enough to touch. Dammit—she spent all these months hating him, hardening her heart, and all it took was one glimpse of him to undo all her work.

The bus lurched as the driver announced her stop through the crackly overhead speakers. Luna made her way to the front exit and as soon as the cold air hit her face, she took a deep breath to get ready for her sprint to work. Emerald Dragon was three blocks away and she was already fifteen minutes late. Mrs. Tan would not be happy.

"I'm sorry!" she said as she breezed through the doors. Brenda Tan, the owner of the restaurant where she worked evenings, gave her a disapproving look from where she stood next to the doorway to the kitchen.

"You're late," the older woman huffed, her eyes narrowing as she watched Luna take her coat off and hang it on the rack.

"The bus was late," Luna muttered.

"Next time you come in late, you're fired," Mrs. Tan threatened in a booming voice that belied her small stature. Luna nodded apologetically and then made her way to the server's station to get ready for her shift. As she put on her apron, she felt a hand on her shoulder.

"Have some tea." Mrs. Tan stood before her, offering her a thermos. Though her brows were drawn in a scowl, her voice was gentle.

"Thank you," she whispered, the metal cylinder slowly warming her hands. Mrs. Tan was a terror, but Luna knew that she had to be otherwise her employees wouldn't respect her. Emerald Dragon had been around for decades and it wasn't just because of the delicious, authentic Cantonese cuisine they served. Mrs. Tan ran a tight ship and didn't hesitate to fire any employee for any misstep. The woman was strict, but she was also fair and Luna had witnessed her generosity on more than one occasion.

"Fetch the new batch of tea in the storeroom for me," Mrs. Tan commanded as another employee scurried by.

"Yes, Mrs. Tan," she answered, knowing what the old woman meant. Going to the storeroom meant an extra five minutes of alone time where she could sit and compose herself. Walking down the hall to the rear of the restaurant, she opened the door to the stock room and made a beeline for the chair near the rack of spices and sauces. Unscrewing the top of the thermos, she took a sip of the tea, the liquid warming her insides, but not calming her.

Dammit to hell. Killian was in New York. Her hands shook as she sat down on the rickety, plastic chair. Luna gulped hard, trying not to let the tears spill down her cheeks. No. She promised herself she wouldn't cry anymore. Not for him. He was responsible for her predicament. For everything. She'd lost her job, her beautiful apartment, her wonderful life, all because of Killian.

How she wished she'd never met him.

That night at the gala when she'd seen the mysterious man looking at the *Gastlava Tapestry*, she'd felt drawn to him. Mustering all her courage, she'd gone over to talk to him. And then she took him around the museum, showing him all her favorite places. God, he was so handsome and charming. And she'd fallen for it; hook, line, and sinker. He'd had no trouble reeling her in.

Of course, she'd resisted at first. It wasn't appropriate for one thing, seeing as Killian's company was supposedly going to be a big donor. It took a few days, of him pursuing her, calling her, coming to visit her at lunchtime until she'd agreed to a date. And of course, she'd slept with him on that first date. They'd barely made it into her apartment.

The bustling sound outside the stock room shook her out of her thoughts, and she stood up, grabbed a bag of tea and headed out. Luna made her way to the front of the restaurant, taking a deep breath to prepare herself mentally for her long shift.

"*Aiyah*, that stupid cook!" Mrs. Tan raved as Luna mopped the floor. Most of the other servers and staff had gone home, but Luna elected to stay a few minutes to make up for the lateness.

"What's wrong, Mrs. Tan?" Luna asked, putting the mop aside.

"That cook made too much fried rice again. So wasteful." She shook her head. "Here," she handed Luna a large paper bag. "Take this home."

"Oh, I couldn't—"

"Take it!" The older woman insisted. "Otherwise, I'll just throw it away."

"Thank you." Luna accepted the bag. This wasn't the first time Mrs. Tan had given her food to take home. It seemed every other week or so, some employee would make a mistake and order too much of something, or someone would cancel delivery whenever Luna would be working. While she initially felt embarrassed, she couldn't say no to free food. Not when her funds were dwindling and she was starving all the damn time.

"Now go home," Mrs. Tan urged, her voice softening. "I'll finish up. Staying out late is not good for—"

"Thank you," she said, interrputing her boss. Turning around, she grabbed her coat and slipped it on. With one last wave to her boss, she left the restaurant and headed towards the bus stop.

The scent of fragrant fried rice rose from the bag and filled her nostrils, making her stomach grumble. She was starving. The last thing she had eaten was the staff meal she'd quickly scarfed down in between serving tables. The rice could last her two meals at least. Well, it could, but she'd probably finish the whole thing in one sitting.

Luna laughed bitterly. *If her mom could see her now.* But, no, she didn't know about what had happened. No one would. She'd moved across the country so no one back home would see how far she had fallen. Sure, she wasn't that high up in the first place.

Julia Rhoades was a struggling single mom who was doing her best to support her daughter when their family imploded. She worked hard to put food on the table by cleaning houses and picking up odd jobs here and there. One day, she'd been lucky enough to have been hired by Mr. and Mrs. Thomas Van Der Meer, a wealthy couple who had no children of their own. They liked Julia so much they invited her to be their full-time housekeeper and to live with them. Luna had grown up in their mansion in Portland's affluent Lake Oswego district. The Van Der Meers took a liking to Luna. Growing up, they'd introduced her to music, art, and culture—things she would never have known as the child of a single mother who cleaned houses. She especially took a liking to art and would spend hours in the extensive library, staring at books filled with paintings by DaVinci, Picasso, Vermeer, and other great artists.

Thanks to the Van Der Meers, she graduated from the Portland Art Institute without any debt. They also introduced her to the curator of the Portland Art Museum who took her on, first as an executive assistant. Luna worked hard, making her own way until finally she became one of the youngest curators in the museum. That's why it was so hard to tell her mother and the Van Der Meers about her fall from grace. She was grateful that her boss was able to keep things out of the papers, otherwise—

The headlights to her right startled her, and she stood there rooted to the spot in the middle of the crosswalk. It happened so fast, the pain barely registering as the car hit her body, sending her flying towards the pavement.

A scream piercing the air. Feet pounding the pavement. Bodies surrounding her. Though her vision blackened, Luna could hear all these sounds, mingled with the constant din of sirens, traffic, and people around her.

"Has someone called 911?"

"Did you get the plate number?"

"It was a Honda, I think. Dark blue. I think the plates were blocked out."

"Motherfuckin' hit and run."

"Bastard."

As Luna opened her eyes, she saw half a dozen figures around her. Who said New Yorkers were indifferent?

"Lady, don't move! The paramedics are on their way."

"Oh, Lord. She's pregnant!"

Luna's hand immediately went to her rounded stomach. She waited for pain, for the sensation of sticky blood on her thighs as she'd seen in all those movies where the woman loses her child after falling down the stairs or slipping on a wet floor. But she felt nothing. She took a deep breath and sat up.

"I said don't move, lady!" one of the bystanders said.

"I'm fine," she assured them. Was she?

"You got hit by a fuckin' car, and you think you're fine?"

"Maybe she hit her head," someone offered. "She's in shock."

Whoever said that was probably right. Luna was in complete shock. She wobbled slightly but was able to get to her feet on her own. Brushing the side of her face, Luna felt the syrupy blood on her fingers. *Gross*. She wiped it on her coat and gently touched her fingers to her face, searching for the wound. But, she found none. In fact, her face was clean—no gashes, no wounds, no cuts, not even a scratch. What the hell was going on?

A movement in her belly made her gasp, and her hands immediately went to her stomach. The baby kicked for the first time! Was he or she okay? Or was this the beginning of a miscarriage? It kicked again as if to tell her that everything was okay.

"The EMTs are almost here!"

"Lady, you need to sit down or something."

"No!" she protested, placing her hands protectively around her stomach. "No doctors. *Please*." She didn't have insurance. The cost of the ambulance ride alone would cripple her financially. She'd been saving every cent she could all these months for the baby. She was all right. Maybe she wasn't hit by a car and she just fell. Yeah—that was it.

"Lady—no! Where are you going?"

"I'm going home," she declared, turning around and walking away from the crowd that had gathered.

"What the fuck, lady?"

"What do you mean, *going home*?"

"Oh, Harold, can you believe it? We have a real New York story to tell when we go back home to St. Louis."

Luna picked up her pace, running towards the first subway entrance she could find. When she got through the turnstiles, she breathed a sigh of relief, knowing for sure no one would follow her. As she stood on the platform, Luna ran her hands all over her body. No broken bones, no sprain, not even a scratch anywhere. She felt okay, maybe a little lightheaded, but no pain at all. What the hell was going on?

Sixteen weeks. She was sixteen weeks pregnant and just got hit by a car, yet she escaped unscathed. When she left Portland, she was flat broke from all the lawyer's fees. No one would hire her on the West Coast, so she went to New York. Her last bit of money went towards bus fare, food, and lodging. There was no money for doctor's visits or vitamins. An old classmate helped her out and put her in touch with a small gallery in New York. They hired her, but only part time and for a massive pay cut with no benefits. Night shifts at the restaurant helped her meager income though it wouldn't be enough by the time the baby came.

And now this. Was there something wrong with her? She laughed out loud, startling the homeless man sitting in the corner. Well, at least she wasn't hurt and didn't need to go to the doctor. She should be grateful and leave it at that, right?

3

"Bye, Boss," Evie said to Killian as she headed out the door.

"Good luck on that audition!" Meredith shouted. "I mean, break a leg. Oh my God, did I just jinx you by wishing you good luck? Oh, fuck nuts, I'm sorry!"

Evie laughed. "No, Meredith, that's for when you're in the theater."

"Oh good," Meredith sighed in relief. "Well, go and kill 'em."

"I will!" With a final wave goodbye, she disappeared.

"Wow, she's only been here two days?" Quinn said as he looked around the office. The boxes and the clutter were gone. The reception area looked like a real office lobby and there was now space for people to sit on the couch. Evie had even rescued a potted tree from the dumpster out back and placed it in the corner.

"Yeah, she's got the magic touch," Killian said. He knew hiring Evie was a good idea. She'd already re-organized the file cabinet, chuckling as she undid Meredith's unique filing system.

"And Connor?" Meredith asked. "Still no sign of him?"

"Where is he staying these days?" Quinn added.

"He's around," was all Killian said.

Truth be told, he wasn't sure. When they moved to New York, they all found their own homes. At least Killian and Quinn did, the latter having bought himself a nice loft in SoHo from his share of Archie's estate. Connor, however, with his restless nature, preferred to stay in hotel rooms, moving every couple of weeks. Killian wasn't sure where he was staying now, but he kept in touch via text. Did Connor really hate Evie that much? Damn, his brother was stubborn, but he was going to have to show his face eventually.

"So, what have you two been up to?" Killian asked, changing the subject.

"I had this hot date last night," Quinn said. "We had dinner at Nobu."

"Daric took me to Paris for dinner," Meredith said smugly.

"You're such a one-upper," Quinn moaned. "We can't all have warlock husbands with super transportation powers, you know."

"You're just jealous my date probably ended better than yours," she retorted. "Did you get lucky at least? At five hundred bucks a pop, dinner at Nobu should warrant you at least a handy."

"I'll have you know—"

A knock on the door followed by the jiggling of the doorknob made all three Lycans stand at attention. Years of training, of always keeping their senses on alert for danger, made them all eerily still and quiet.

Meredith pointed to the door indicating she would open it. Good idea. A woman might make an intruder let down his guard which would make him easier to disable. Killian nodded and stood to the right of the door while Quinn planted himself on the opposite side.

Killian watched closely as Meredith turned the knob. The

door swung open to the left side which meant he couldn't see who it was.

"Can I help you?" Meredith asked.

"Where is Killian? I need to see him."

That voice. *No. It couldn't be.*

"Who are you? Hey, you can't come in here!"

Killian held his breath, waiting for what would happen next and then there she was, standing in the middle of his reception area. Luna Rhoades. She was wearing a black coat, and her beanie had gone askew over her head. Her platinum blonde locks now stopped short at her jawline, and he realized it *was* her he'd seen the other day. Did she see him? Follow him back to the office? What did she want?

"Where is he? I need to see him now," she said. "I need to—"

"I'm here, Luna," he said, barely able to get the words out. Hate filled his veins like ice. Yet, he couldn't form the words 'I hate you', not even in his mind.

Luna's violet eyes grew wide when they landed on Killian. He didn't miss the dark smudges under them nor the unusual pallor on her sunken cheeks. If she'd been miserable any time during the past four months, then she deserved every goddamn second of it.

"Killian," she said breathlessly.

"What are you doing here?" He crossed his arms over his chest. "How did you find me?"

"I saw you the other day by Union Square," she said. "So I waited for you this morning and followed you back here."

Killian gritted his teeth. After the day he thought he saw Luna, he couldn't help but pass by Union Square every single chance he got. He told himself it was just to make sure she'd been a figment of his imagination.

"You know her?" Meredith asked.

He ignored the shock and surprise on his siblings' faces.

"Tell me what you want and then get out," Killian said in a cool voice.

"What did you do to me?" Luna asked when she finally spoke. "You did something to me, and now I'm a freak!"

"What the hell are you talking about? I haven't seen you in four months." Killian felt his blood boiling. She was the one who walked away from what they could have had. And now she was accusing him of doing something to her?

"It's the only explanation why I'm like this!" she shouted. She withdrew something from the pocket of her coat. Metal glinted in her hands.

"*Jesus Christ*," Quinn exclaimed as he stepped forward. "Put that thing away before you hurt someone, doll."

Luna held up the knife and pointed it at Quinn. "Stay away."

Quinn rolled his eyes and continued to advance. Luna's scent, thick with fear filled the air and Killian held his hand up.

"Quinn—no."

"But she can't hurt me—"

"I said no," he commanded and Quinn stopped in his tracks. "Luna," he began. "Put the knife down and we'll talk."

"Talk?" she cried. "*Talk?* Okay, let's talk. You can explain to me what this is about."

"No!" Meredith screeched as Luna held the knife to her wrist and slit the delicate skin there.

His inner wolf howled. On instinct, Killian leaped forward and made a grab for Luna, but she quickly evaded him. "Are you insane?" he growled as he turned around to face her. "What the fuck were you thinking?"

"Look." Luna held her hand out showing them her wrist. Blood dripped down from her wrist, but there was no wound. The skin was completely healed.

Meredith gasped. "Oh, my God."

"What is happening to me, Killian?" Luna asked in a frantic

voice. "I...I tried everything. I mean, I got hit by a car the other night. And then...I don't know, I thought it was strange that nothing happened to me. Then last night I tried to cut my hand, but it kept healing, over and over again, no matter how many times I tried. I've racked my brain to find an answer until I realized there's only one explanation."

Killian didn't know what to say. Couldn't say anything. So Meredith spoke up.

"Honey," she soothed, moving closer to her. "Give me the knife."

"No."

"Please. Give it to me and I'll explain. I'll tell you what's happening to you."

Luna's expression of determination faltered and she held her hand out, the blade pointing towards Meredith who grasped it, her fingers wrapped around the sharp edge before dragging her hand deliberately along the length of it .

"No!" Luna yelled and pulled the knife away, letting it fall to the ground. "Why did you do that?"

Meredith held her hand up. Although smeared with blood, there was no wound on her palms. "See? I know what's 'wrong' with you. I have it too."

Luna looked relieved, her arms falling limply to her sides. "What's wrong with us? Are we sick?"

"No," Meredith shook her head and looked at Killian meaningfully. "It's our babies. Protecting us from harm. We're invincible. That's what happens when we become pregnant with our True Mate's child."

Luna collapsed to the floor.

---

3 Months Ago...

Killian never thought of himself as a one-woman kind of man, but Luna made him entertain dangerous thoughts that veered towards just that. Commitment. Rings. Forever. Hell, he was practically there already. He hadn't even looked at another woman since he met Luna. Quinn was disappointed that he'd lost his best wingman.

But he couldn't deny that he was deliriously happy.

After that first date, he spent nearly every free moment he had with Luna. Taking her to lunch; dinners at her place, and of course, making love to her every chance he got. He thought all he needed was one night to get her out of his system, but he only wanted her more each time. Luna was beautiful and gorgeous, yes, but she was also passionate and giving, matching him in every way.

The rest of his time was taken up with the job. Trying to find a way to steal the *Gastlava Tapestry* was more challenging than he'd thought. He was running out of time and options. Unfortunately, as he grew more desperate, it seemed there was only one option available to him. Luna.

He didn't set out to chase after her just because she was a curator at the museum. The attraction between them that first night was undeniable and he knew he had to have her. Of course, he couldn't help it that he spent a lot of time there now they were dating. It gave him an excuse to scope out the place and assess the security without bringing about any suspicion. The guards all knew him and didn't bat an eye when he strolled into the office looking for Luna. His naturally observant nature immediately picked up on the keycard she used to open the door to the office when he would bring her to work in the morning. Memorizing the guards' rotation duty and usual routes they took when patrolling the galleries during the day was a snap, as was making a note about the peak times of day and when it was least crowded during the week.

The guilt wrapped around his heart like a vice, but he had a job to do. The Mornavian Government and their people were counting on him to bring their treasure home. He told himself that although Luna never explicitly said she would prefer the tapestry went back to its rightful owners, he knew that's how she felt. They had long conversations about art and politics, and this strong, beautiful woman had convictions that ran deep. She believed in doing what was right.

Killian made the decision. He would have to be careful though and decided that in the days after he stole the tapestry, he would lay low—keep the heat off her. Right before he planned to pull off the heist, he was careful to make himself scarce around the museum. The month of the exhibit was nearly up and he had to move fast.

But of course, life always threw curve balls and this time it was a big one.

"I'm pregnant," Luna blurted out as they lay in each other's arms, sweaty and tired from another intense lovemaking session.

Pregnant? How could that be? Killian didn't grow up in a Lycan clan, but he knew that their kind had problems reproducing. Archie had been married to a Lycan for years and never had any children, no matter how much they tried. He never bothered with condoms when he had sex with Luna and she didn't protest, so he assumed she was on birth control. His inner wolf, on the other hand, relished the thought of a pup. No—not a pup of course. Only two Lycans could produce another Lycan. Any child he would have with Luna would be human.

"Killian? Are you mad?" Her voice was small. He didn't answer back and she stiffened, but when she tried to disentangle herself he clamped his arms around her.

"I'm not mad. Just surprised."

"Why aren't you asking if it's yours?"

"Of course it's mine." He would kill anyone who touched her, and his inner wolf agreed.

She relaxed against him. "I'm scared."

"Don't be, sweetheart." He kissed her on the forehead. "It will be okay."

He wanted to believe that, but a child *would* complicate things. They didn't talk about the baby again for the rest of the night and the following day after he had brought Luna to work, he went to the only man he could talk to about these things: Archie.

The old man's reaction went swiftly from shock to happiness. He seemed ecstatic that he was going to be a grandfather, but agreed that it wasn't going to make his plans easy.

"What are you going to do?" he asked as he poured Killian a glass of his best whiskey.

"Move her into my place. Put my ring on her finger. Raise our baby together."

"I know that. But what about the job?"

He had no choice. The exhibit was closing in two days. He had to move fast, and so he did. With Luna's keycard, he was able to get into the museum after hours. He stole the tapestry and hid it then decided to lay low for a while. It was a week later when he hadn't heard anything in the press about the theft that he thought he was in the clear. But he was wrong.

And everything turned to shit.

4

Meredith and Quinn moved to catch Luna as she fell, but Killian was faster. Her delicious scent filled his nostrils, sending desire straight to his groin. He suppressed a groan, lifted her up and walked over to the couch. As he laid her down, he untied the wool coat and let it fall open.

There it was. The evidence that Killian hadn't imagined that month he spent with her. The bump was evident on her slight frame, making it seem much bigger than the four months since that first night. Yes, if he calculated correctly, that was how far along she was.

"Christ on a cracker, Killian!" Meredith exclaimed when her eyes zeroed in on Luna's pregnant belly. "What's going on? Who is she and why does she have your bun in her oven?"

"Shit," Killian ran his fingers through his hair. "This is Luna. Luna Rhoades."

"How did you get her pregnant?" Quinn asked.

"I think we all know how, Quinn," Meredith quipped.

"I mean," Quinn shot back. "He can't have been that lucky. You know we can't knock up anyone easily."

"Have you not been listening or watching, Quinn?" she

asked in an exasperated voice. "Luna is Killian's True Mate. That means the first time they bumped uglies, his soul mate sperm sped down the uterus express and went to town on that egg. But why aren't you together?"

"It's a long story," Killian said.

"You didn't know, did you?" Meredith deduced. "She didn't tell you she was pregnant."

"She did."

"What?" Quinn yelped, his expression clouded in anger. "You knew she was pregnant, and you left her anyway? How could you leave her?" His brother held his hands in tight fists at his side and his eyes began to glow, signaling his wolf was ready to burst from his skin.

"Chill, Quinn," Meredith soothed, rubbing a palm along his arm. "I'm sure there's a good explanation for this. Right, Killian?"

He wished there were. Before he could speak, Luna began to stir.

Thick lashes fluttered open and her pink lips parted in a soft gasp. Her hands dropped to her belly, feeling the bump there and then she let out a sigh of relief. Amethyst eyes stared up at the ceiling before finding Killian.

"Killian," she murmured. "What's happening to me?"

What should he say? Luna was human and didn't know about shifters. He couldn't tell her all those months ago—not when he was sworn to keep the secret. If they had gotten married or moved in together, he would have had to petition the High Council for permission to tell her and have her pledge to the Lycans. Currently, the Lycan High Council was in shambles thanks to a traitor who had infiltrated them. Still, he didn't know what to do or say now.

"Luna," Meredith said as she knelt down next to the couch. "I'll try to explain."

"Are we sick? Is my baby going to be okay?" Her lips and chin trembled.

Meredith shook her head. "No—everything's going to be all right. I'm Meredith, Killian's sister."

"You said it's happening to you too. This sickness?"

"Er, sort of. It's kind of like a genetic condition. But don't worry, your baby is safe."

Good save, Killian thought. Hopefully, it would buy them time.

"Now, why don't you tell us what you're doing here? Where did you meet Killian? Do you live here?"

"That's not important now," Killian said to Meredith then turned to Luna. "But we do need to talk."

Luna sat up awkwardly, planting her feet on the carpet, her hands wringing on her lap. Her head was bowed and her breathing uneven.

"Killian," Meredith began. "Can I talk to you first?"

"Yeah, we gotta talk," Quinn interjected, his voice edgy.

"Quinn, go get Luna a water or juice, will you? She looks like she's going to faint again," Meredith ordered.

The other Lycan's gaze moved from Luna to Killian, alternating in pity and anger, but he nodded and left the office.

"Just stay put for a second, Luna, while Killian and I talk privately." Meredith tugged on Killian's arm and led him back to his office. When the door closed behind them, she crossed her arms over her chest and pinned him with her gaze. "Explain."

Where to begin? Killian let out a deep sigh and gave Meredith the quickest version he could muster, at least up until the time she told Killian she was pregnant. What happened after...it hurt too much to say out loud. Shock and disbelief were still running through his system, not to mention he was battling his inner wolf. It was in a rage—pacing and howling, slashing at his insides. It was like the wolf was mad at him for keeping him from his pup.

"You didn't know she was your True Mate?"

"How could I, Mer?" he shot back defensively. "Did you know Daric was your True Mate when you met him?" True Mates were rare. In fact, they were virtually unheard of until over a year ago when the first pairing emerged.

"But why did you leave her when she told you she was pregnant? Even after the job?"

"I didn't want to leave her!"

"Then what happened?"

Killian gritted his teeth, his nails digging into his palms so hard he feared it would break the skin. "I finished the job. I used her keycard to get into the museum, making it seem like someone had stolen it from her car." He paused, running his hand over his face. "After I had got the tapestry I laid low. When I came back, she figured it all out somehow and I confessed. She told me she hated me and that she got rid of the baby!" A low growl escaped from his throat. "She killed our baby because she couldn't stand to have it inside her, reminding her of me. That's what she told me."

Meredith's face went completely white and moisture filled her eyes. "Killian, I'm sorry. So that's what you've been keeping from me. From all of us this whole time."

The lump in his throat refused to go away and he was grateful for the door to his office slamming open so he didn't have to answer her.

"What?" he barked at Quinn, who stood in the doorway.

"She's gone," Quinn replied. "I went to the vending machine to get her some juice and when I came back, she wasn't there."

"Dammit!" Meredith cursed. "What if she goes crazy and tells someone? Or she goes to a doctor? Our secret could get out!"

"Fuck!" Killian punched the wall, leaving a dent in the plaster. "I'm going after her."

"I'm coming with you," Meredith said.

"No," he protested. "I have to do this alone."

"You're not in the right mind," she stated. "I can help smooth things over, and maybe buy us more time until we get to talk to Grant Anderson."

Shit, she was right. They would have to tell the Alpha of New York what happened. "Fine. Quinn," he said to his brother. "You stay here and see if you can find her current address in New York."

"Will do. And Killian?"

"Yeah?"

"I'm sorry I got mad at you. I heard what you said—what she told you," he said somberly. "You know I always got your back, bro."

He gave Quinn a curt nod. Truthfully, he wasn't mad that Quinn took Luna's side. From what he knew about Quinn's childhood, he expected that reaction.

"Let's go," he said to Meredith.

---

2 months and 3 weeks ago...

When people describe bad things happening to them, they always say things like they felt their entire world was falling apart. Luna never understood what that meant, but now she understood it all too well. As she left the police station she wanted to collapse, her knees so weak it was like the earth was crumbling underneath her feet.

Bracing herself against a street lamppost, she took a deep breath.

Was it just hours ago that everything seemed bright? Killian had been away on business for almost a week, but they'd been texting regularly. Of course things at work were chaotic, but when she saw his messages, she couldn't help but feel that flutter in her heart that made her forget about everything. She spent whatever free time she had reading baby books and browsing for baby stuff on websites, as well as dreaming of what their child would look like. A girl with Killian's turquoise eyes. Or a boy with his killer smile. Hopefully, he'd be back soon from his trip because she couldn't wait to see him.

When she got to work that morning she had a strange feeling; an uncomfortable pit in her stomach. She ignored it initially, but when she spied the two men in suits waiting outside her office the hole grew even bigger. Jordan and Heathcliff, the detectives from the Portland PD investigating the theft of the *Gastlava Tapestry*, wanted to bring her down to the station to 'talk'.

Luna agreed of course, and followed them down to their HQ, but she should have known. She should have asked for a lawyer or even asked them if she was under arrest and refused to come. But hindsight is always 20/20, and Luna had never suspected they were after her.

They put her in a small room with a mirror and asked her questions one after the other. Yes, she knew her access card was stolen. Yes, she left it in her briefcase in the car which someone had broken into. No, she didn't report it right away because it was the weekend. No, she didn't go anywhere that weekend; she stayed home, alone.

Finally, after what seemed like hours, they dropped the bomb. At first they said there was no way they could prove she had anything to do with it and they were going to drop the criminal investigation. However, Larry Bakersfield was going to file a civil suit against her and the museum so she had better find a good lawyer.

She thought that was that, but of course there was more bad news. Her boss called and said they were going to have to let her go for negligence. They didn't even want to let her come to the office and told her that they would send her personal items on. Perhaps she should be glad she didn't have to go back to the museum, knowing her boss and coworkers thought she had something to do with the theft.

Luna somehow made it home from the police station without breaking down. She immediately got on her computer and started looking for a good lawyer. They cost an arm and a leg, but what could she do? She didn't have a choice.

Luna tossed and turned the entire night. Trying to retrace her steps and going over in her mind how she lost that access card. She last used it the day before the theft to enter the office and took it everywhere. Killian couldn't have lunch that day. In fact, he was hardly coming by to see her during the day anymore, but she had dinner every night with him and then they stayed at her place. Hmmm,...she had never been to his apartment, even after a month but never thought anything of it. He mentioned having a place in the city but had omitted saying where.

She brushed those thoughts aside for now. The access card — that was what was important. She had to figure out what happened to it so she could clear her name. Clearing her mind of everything but that day, she thought back to that morning.

After waking up, she showered and dressed, kissed Killian goodbye, and went to work. She used the keycard to get into the office and then dropped it in her briefcase. Following a meeting at ten o'clock, she went to lunch and finished her work. At the end of the day, she met with Killian at a lovely, little French place by the waterfront. After dinner, they took a stroll around the river and walked back to the parking lot. Unfortunately, when they got back to her car, the rear passenger window had been smashed, and her briefcase had been stolen from the back.

Oh, she felt so stupid! Why did she leave her bag there? Killian consoled her, told her there was nothing she could do. Luna wanted to go to the police to file a report, but Killian said it could wait until Monday. There was no way she was going to get it back anyway and at least her car was still there. Being tired, all she wanted to do was go back home and snuggle with Killian under the covers, so she agreed.

Did someone take her briefcase to get her keycard to steal the tapestry? It couldn't have been a crime of opportunity. The *Gastalava Tapestry* had some serious security around it, and whoever stole it was a pro. The access card allowed them to bypass the main museum security system and avoid setting off the alarms.

There was niggling feeling in her brain, one that wouldn't leave her alone, preventing her from sleep. As the sun rose outside her window, she got up and went to her computer. She pulled up her web search engine and entered 'Grover Real Estates Holdings'. Up popped the company website and a couple of pages, but nothing else. No news sites, trade publications or even prominent real estate blogs. She clicked on the company's page and went to the contact form. Grabbing her phone from her bedside table, she dialed the number listed, but all she heard was a recorded message saying the number wasn't in service. She tried again, but it was the same message.

Her heart drummed in her chest and that hole in her stomach came back. No. They must have had the wrong number listed on their website. She tried Killian's number, but it was busy. He was in Europe on business and it was in the middle of the night there. How could his number be busy?

The pressure behind her eyes was building and she clutched at her stomach. Was he really in Europe? Was he really even Vice President of Grover Real Estates Holding? Or did he make that all up? She felt nauseous the whole day and it wasn't just morning sickness. Her mouth felt like sand and everything she tried to eat had no taste. In the afternoon, her phone buzzed with a text from Killian greeting her good morning and telling her about the lovely breakfast he was having on his terrace in Madrid.

Luna wanted to scream and throw the phone against the wall. Or should she call him back and tell him he was a liar? Instead, she ignored him. When she didn't answer back, more texts arrived. Unable to control herself, she glanced at the screen.

What's wrong baby?

R u ok?

Text me back now.

Then the calls came, one right after the other and she let all of them go to voicemail. When she couldn't stand it anymore, she tossed the phone out of the window and dove into bed, burying her face in the pillow and letting out a scream.

For two days and nights, Luna holed up in her apartment. She couldn't sleep, her mind reeling from all that was happening. She was pregnant and jobless. She spoke with a lawyer and when he told her the final figure of what it might cost to defend her, she wanted to be sick. She would probably have to sell her apartment—her beautiful home that she'd worked so hard for. What would she tell her mom and the Van der Meers? Could she even get a job after this whole thing was over?

She was running out of food and she didn't want to get delivery anymore, so Luna decided to go and get some groceries. As she left the lobby of her building, she bumped into something hard and solid. The scent of rain was unmistakable.

"*Luna*," Killian cried, wrapping his arms around her. "Thank God you're okay. I thought something had happened to you when you didn't answer my texts. Please don't do that again."

The anger she'd repressed had been slowly bubbling up like a geyser. And now, faced with the subject of her rage, she let it explode like Old Faithful.

"*You fucking asshole.*" She pushed against him and must have caught him by surprise because he stumbled back. "You did it, didn't you?"

"Sweetheart, I don't know—"

"Shut up! Stop lying to me." She stood there looking up at him, her eyes blazing. "You stole my access card and tried to hide it by staging a break-in. And then you used my card to get into the museum to steal the tapestry."

Killian's face was blank, his firm lips drawn into a tight line. As the silence drew out, the tension between them grew thicker.

His shoulders sagged. "Yes," he finally confessed. "I did. I'm so sorry, Luna."

Hate, rage, disgust, and revulsion swirled inside her and her vision clouded. "You *bastard*. Not only are you a liar, but you're a thief, too. Tell me—was seducing me part of your plan? Did you have to think of someone else while you were fucking me? Or was it all worth it? Just how many millions did you get for the tapestry anyway?"

"Luna, stop. Please listen to me." He tried to put his hand on her shoulder, but she shrugged him off. "It's not like that!"

"No! Don't you dare touch me. I can't stand being around you. I hate you." She turned around and began to walk back into her apartment building.

"Luna, let me explain. I didn't mean to hurt you, *please*." He grabbed her wrist. "Please listen to me. I want to be with you. And our baby."

The thought of Killian touching her again and her child

made her insides turn. Growing up, Luna had never known her father, but one day her mother told her the truth—he was serving a life sentence in prison for killing a police officer. No— her child would never have a criminal for a father. Not like she had growing up, leaving her mother to raise her alone. She could do it, too. For the sake of her child, she *had* to do it. Pivoting back, she looked at him so that she could say it to his face.

"There is no baby," she said, the lie sliding smoothly from her mouth.

"What do you mean? Are you hurt? Did you have a miscarriage?"

"No."

His hand released her wrist and dropped to his side. The concern on his face melted away, replaced by a cold mask. "Why?" he rasped.

"Because I hate you," she whispered. "I hate you and I couldn't stand the thought of having your baby inside me. You ruined my life, Killian, and I never want to see you again."

5

Luna was still pregnant.

The baby he thought was long gone was still inside her. The memory of that day played on replay constantly in his mind and kept him up most nights. It pushed his wolf to the breaking point, and he had feared the animal would go insane and break free from his skin. There wasn't a day that went by that he didn't think about the loss. And now that she was here and the baby was still there, he could hardly believe it. It felt like waking from a nightmare that never ended.

He couldn't even bring himself to be mad at Luna, not when it felt like a vice that had been wrapped around his heart was now loosening. He had to find her before she left again.

Even though New York was a city of millions of people, it wasn't hard for Killian to track Luna down. He had her scent memorized, etched so permanently into his brain that it was easy enough to follow the trail once he caught it. The inner wolf inside him was eager to find her too, sniffing for the lingering smell of sugar and cinnamon in the air.

Being on foot, she hadn't gone far. Killian and Meredith caught up with her a mere couple of streets from the office.

They followed her block after block until they reached the edge of the East Village. She stopped in front of an old building, fumbled for her keys and went inside.

"What the hell is she doing here?"

"She obviously lives here, *duh*," Meredith said.

"Why would she live in a place like this?" His mind raced with questions. Luna had a gorgeous apartment in Portland. She loved that place and judging from the way she'd decorated it, it was obviously her pride and joy. So why then was she staying in a dump like this? Even if she'd sold her place, she could have afforded something much better with the profits. And it wasn't like her parents were hard up for cash either if she'd needed any. One weekend, when she said she couldn't stay over because she was going home to see family, curiosity had gotten the better of him. He followed her all the way to a beautiful mansion on the lake. There was no way parents who lived like that would let their daughter stay here.

Meredith shrugged. "The rent in Manhattan is too damn high, that's why. Well—at least we know where she lives now. Should we stake her place out and make sure she doesn't go telling anyone?"

"I'm going in after her," he declared. "I need to get to the bottom of this."

"You can't. What are you going to do, break into her apartment? Killian, wait—*Killian*."

He was already halfway across the street when he heard Meredith grumbling behind him. Jogging up the stoop, he bent and examined the door. Jesus Christ, what kind of security was this? The door knob was older than him. He took his lock picking tool from his pocket and slipped it into the keyhole. It opened in three seconds, and the ancient wood heaved and creaked when he pushed it.

"What a dump," Meredith declared.

Killian agreed. There were newspapers piled in one corner, dirty bottles strewn about, and the damp smell of mold in the air was unmistakable. He checked the mailboxes but didn't see Luna's name. The mixed cooking smells in the confined space were blocking his senses so he couldn't follow her scent. Shit. Maybe they could knock on every door until they found her.

"Let me help you, ma'am."

He turned at Meredith's voice to find her holding the door of the building open for an elderly woman.

"Oh, thank you, dear," the woman said when she made it all the way in. "It's nice that young people know how to respect their elders."

"It's what my grandma taught me," Meredith replied cheerfully. "Say, ma'am, I was wondering if you could help me. I'm here to surprise my sister, Luna. Luna Rhoades. But I seem to have forgotten her apartment number. I can't remember if it's 1B or 2B—and I can't call her or I'll ruin the surprise."

"Oh. Luna, yes," she replied, her cloudy eyes brightening in recognition. "Pretty young thing with blonde hair? That girl, she's always exhausted from working at that restaurant in Chinatown, you know? But she always has time to check on me every other morning. Asks me if I need anything. Maybe to check if I'm still alive," she chuckled. "I don't have any family and my dear Marlow passed away fifteen years ago. My children don't even call—"

"Uh, ma'am?" Meredith interrupted gently. "Her apartment?"

"Oh! Yes, I'm sorry dear, I do tend to ramble on. It's...." She trailed off, her eyes looking into the distance. "It's 2C, I believe."

"Thank you!"

Killian strode to the stairs, taking them two at a time to the second floor.

"What exactly are you going to do?" Meredith asked when

she caught up. "Look, I bought us some time, we know where she lives, and Quinn can probably find out where she works. Let's go back and talk to the Alpha. He'll know what to do."

He ignored her and kept walking towards the apartment. He stopped when he reached the door, contemplating whether he should just pick the lock or knock.

"Killian, for fuck's sake," Meredith said in an exasperated voice. "Don't you do it."

"I have to," he replied, before knocking on the door. His knuckles rapped sharply on the wood. No answer. He knocked again. "Luna!" he called. "I know you're in there."

"That woman was older than this building. She might have given us the wrong apartment number," Meredith pointed out.

Before he could answer her, the door opened, and Luna's face appeared. "What are you doing here?" she asked her eyes wide as saucers. "Don't you—*what do you think you're doing?*"

Killian barged into her apartment, ignoring her protests. "Hey, you can't just come in here!" she exclaimed, her cheeks puffing out in anger.

"What the hell are you doing here, Luna?" he asked, looking around. While the apartment was clean, it was also cramped. The three of them could barely fit inside. A shabby futon was pushed up against a wall and next to it was a side table with a laptop. On the opposite end was the small kitchen, though really, that was being generous. The room consisted of a counter with a hot plate and a sink, plus a few dishes stacked neatly on the side. There was a single door next to the mini fridge that was either a closet or a bathroom.

"I live here," she retorted. "Now get out or I'll call the cops."

"Why the fuck are you living in this hellhole?" Killian couldn't help himself. His brain couldn't reconcile what he was seeing. His inner wolf, on the other hand, was starting to get antsy.

"It's all I can afford," she answered, her face growing red with embarrassment. "Now that you're done insulting my home, you can go."

"What about your apartment in Portland? Or the mansion on Lake Oswego? Why aren't your parents supporting you?"

"The mansion? How—Did you follow me to the Van der Meer's mansion?" Her face twisted in anger.

"You mean your family's home? That's what you said, right? You were going home to see some family?"

"Not that it's any of your business," she stated, putting her hands on her hips. "I did grow up in that house, but it wasn't my family's. My mother was the housekeeper, and we lived there with the wealthy couple who owned it."

The blood pounding in Killian's ears was making him dizzy and his body was as stiff as a board. All this time he'd thought she was some rich, spoiled princess. "And your apartment?"

Luna's face fell and he wished he hadn't asked. She took a deep breath. "I had to sell it. Lawyers aren't cheap, you know."

"But they didn't charge you," he said in a daze. "I checked. The Portland PD never charged anyone."

"Yeah, well that didn't stop Larry Bakersfield from suing me in civil court," Luna huffed. "Oh, that case got thrown out, but not before I spent every cent I had defending myself. By the end of it, I was flat broke and no one would hire me. The bastard blackballed me from every gallery on the West Coast. The only place that would hire me was a small artist community here in New York, and even that's part time and has no benefits."

"Luna..." He couldn't say anything, not with the battle raging inside him. His inner wolf was angry. No, it was furious. Furious at him for not protecting Luna, for not taking care of her. He looked at her; at the hollows of her cheeks and the dark smudges under her eyes. Her arms were thin—much thinner than he'd remembered. In fact her entire body was skinnier, save for the protruding bump of her belly. She had been miserable, all right. Miserable and starving—because of him.

Luna let out a sharp cry and clutched at her stomach through the thin, white t-shirt she wore. Killian moved towards her, but she raised a hand. "Don't touch me!" she yelled as she sank down on the futon.

He stilled, rooted to where he stood like a tree. "Why did you tell me you got rid of it? I'm the father. I have a right to know my child."

"Did you really think I could have an abortion?" she accused, tears pooling in her eyes. "Yes, I lied to you about that. But there was something I wasn't lying about. I hate you, Killian. Or whoever the hell you are. I hate you, and I will burn the world before I let you into this child's life. Now," she stood up, her eyes full of fury. "*Get out.*"

Killian was silent, her words sinking slowly into him.

"Killian," Meredith called softly,. "Let's go."

What could he do? Meekly, he followed his sister out of the apartment.

"I didn't know," Killian said as they walked down the stoop. "I swear, she wasn't supposed to get hurt. I made sure."

"You couldn't have planned this," Meredith assured him. "You couldn't have known."

"But I should have!" he roared. The wolf was screaming to get out—to take over his skin and bleed something.

"Jesus, calm down Killian!" Meredith's eyes began to glow, a sign that her wolf was sensing just how close he was to losing control.

"I gotta go," he shouted as he began to walk away from Meredith. He needed to be alone.

Killian wasn't sure how he got home. Did he run over twenty blocks to his condo? Get in a cab, a bus, or subway? He didn't know. As soon as he slammed the door shut behind him, the wolf shredded its way to the surface, tearing his clothes to ribbons. It proceeded to rip apart everything it could get its claws and teeth on—the couch, his coffee table, the lamp—even the carpets. He thought the wolf was done with the living room, but it stalked to his bedroom and tore at his bedsheets, slashing its massive claws across the wooden headboard.

At some point, he blacked out and woke in the middle of the night on the floor of the living room. He didn't even want to survey the damage. Whatever it was, however bad, he deserved it. He was a fucking bastard.

Of course Luna hated him. He left her to deal with his shit. And now she was pregnant, alone and broke. No, he would take care of that. He would take care of her and his child and spend the rest of his life trying to make it up to her. She was his True Mate and they were meant to be together. The first thing he would do was to move her out of that apartment and into his condo. Not that his place was any better right this moment, but he'd get some cleaners in the morning and buy some new furniture.

"What the fuck did you do?"

It was dark, but he knew that voice. "Connor," he said. "I'm redecorating. Like what I've done with the place?"

His brother let out a huff that sounded like a laugh. Connor leaned down and gave him a hand, which he took gratefully. "Thanks. Where have you been?" he asked as he got to his feet.

"Around," Connor replied. "Meredith called me. Said you were in trouble." He lifted his other hand which was holding up a six pack of beer. "You know I'm not much for talking, but I'm good at keeping quiet and pretending to listen."

Killian chuckled. "Fine. Sit on the couch. I think there's a spot that's not too damaged."

Connor eased down onto the broken couch gingerly, probably worried his large frame would make the frail piece of furniture collapse. He heaved a sigh when it seemed to hold up.

Killian sat on the love seat, the one piece that had escaped the wolf's rage. He popped open the beer and told Connor everything, from the time he got the job to a few hours ago when he followed Luna home.

"And Archie knew?" Connor asked. "Why didn't he do anything? Help you? You should have talked to him."

"That day I came out of hiding and Luna told me she got an abortion was the same day we got a call from NYPD. When they found Archie's body."

Connor said nothing, but let out a grunt.

Killian now wondered what would have happened if he didn't leave for New York. Putting an entire country between him and Luna seemed like a good idea at that time. He was barely hanging on, the thought of losing his child driving him and his wolf mad. What if he had stayed? Would he have heard about the civil case? Would he have seen Luna around town obviously pregnant and figured it out? Or would he have broken down and gone to see her anyway and discovered she didn't have an abortion? So many what ifs.

"Whatcha gonna do, brother?" Connor asked.

He let out a sigh. "Luna is mine. They're both mine and I'm going to do what it takes to get them back."

"You gonna tell her what we are?"

"I have to. She'll figure it out. Hopefully, I can tell her before the kid hits puberty."

"Aw, shit, Killian," Connor let out a real laugh. "You're gonna be a daddy."

That truth had been staring him in the face the whole day, but the realization only hit him now. *Daddy. A kid. A pup.* "Fuck." He needed to make this right. Maybe take a bit of time off. Sebastian would understand with a kid on the way himself. No more extended ops overseas. "Connor, I need you."

"Whatever you want, you know you got it."

"Good—because I need you to be in the office more."

"No fucking way," Connor groused.

"Whatever is going on with you, just work through it or put it aside until I can fix this Luna thing? Please?"

Connor let out a growl and frowned, making the scar on his face etch deeper into his face. "Fine. I'll be around more."

"Good."

"But don't ask me to sign papers or do expense accounts. You know I hate that shit."

"You hate everything, Connor," he pointed out.

"Damn right I do."

6

"Here you go. Lemon chicken," Luna said cheerfully as she laid the fragrant dish on the table. "And some beef broccoli for you." She wiped her sticky hands on her apron and smiled down at the older couple. "Anything else I can get for you?"

"No, dear, thank you," the woman said. Her eyes immediately dropped to her belly. "When are you due? Is it a boy or girl? What do you plan to name him or her?"

A pained expression flashed briefly on her face, but Luna immediately replaced it with a fake smile. "*Uhm...*"

"You don't need to answer that," the man said. "Sorry, my wife's a little nosy."

"I'm just asking," the woman huffed in indignation.

"It's all right," Luna assured her. "I'm due in about twenty-two weeks. And as for the sex, I'm not sure yet."

"Ah, you want it to be a surprise. Good for you! I'm sure you and your husband will be happy to have a healthy baby."

Luna gave her a tight smile, nodded her thanks, and turned away before they could see the sadness on her face. She checked her other tables, made sure they didn't need her, and then went to the corner to sit down on the chair Mrs. Tan had placed there so she could take a breather between trips to her tables.

Well, the truth was finally out. Luna felt as if a massive weight had lifted from her shoulders, but now what? Would Killian try to take the baby away? Sue her for custody? He was obviously doing well for himself and Luna wouldn't be able to afford a lawyer. How dare he come to her home and insult her? She was doing much better now at least.

The first week she arrived in New York, she'd had to sleep on a mattress on the floor in an apartment in Greenwich Village which she shared with two students from Cambodia. She used the last of her money to put the deposit for her apartment in the East Village and moved in as soon as she could.

The other thing that made her sigh with relief was the fact that her baby was okay. It seemed strange what was happening to her, but Killian's sister seemed healthy enough. Meredith didn't seem pregnant, though the woman was much taller than her, so she probably carried it better.

Killian. He had this whole family she never knew about. What was this genetic disease they all had? Would her baby have it, too? She somehow had to find a way to scrape together the money for a doctor's visit.

A dinging sound by the kitchen door told her that her next order was up. She got to her feet and retrieved the tray of hot food then proceeded with her shift on full automatic mode. Luna had been doing this for two months after all, and she knew how to plaster the smile on her face and serve food. Tips had never been a problem especially after she started showing. A lot of the diners were generous to the pregnant waitress and tonight, she just might have enough money to treat herself to a burger and large fries after her shift.

When the last table was wiped clean and utensils put away,

Luna put on her coat and waved goodbye to her coworkers and Mrs. Tan, then braced herself for the chilly weather.

The news had predicted a snow storm tonight, probably half a foot by morning and the flakes were already starting to fall from the sky. Luna had always loved the winter growing up, especially when the snow would cover the lakeside. She and her mom shared a small suite in the Van der Meer's mansion and though her room was small, it had the best view of the lake.

Luna stopped for a moment, closing her eyes, just to concentrate on the feel of the flakes melting on her cheeks. She turned her face skywards, enjoying the sensation and forgetting for the moment that her life was in the toilet.

"Well, well, what do we have here?"

Luna's thoughts snapped back to earth. It was dark and she thought she had been walking alone, but she was wrong. Three men stopped in front of her, their faces obscured by the shadows of the building around her. They were all large though, from what she could see. Much taller and broader than her and they were taking up the entire sidewalk.

"Excuse me," she whispered as she motioned to get by them.

"Where ya going?" one of them asked.

"I'm going home," she replied in a much firmer voice.

"I don't think so," the one in the middle said.

What the hell? But before she could protest, a pair of hands grabbed at her arms. Fearing for her and her child's life, Luna let out a piercing scream. A large palm slapped her and then muffled her mouth.

"Make another sound and I'm gonna do more than smack you around, ya hear?" the man who hit her said. "Dammit, Kurt. You're supposed to wait for us to shut her up before making a grab for her."

"She was going to get away," Kurt, the one who was holding her arm, protested.

"You idiot, she's five-foot nuthin' and with that thing in her belly, she'd never get far. The client said no complications. And cops are complications."

Dear God, what was happening? Was she being kidnapped? Did they know about the Van der Meers? Thomas and Carla loved her like one of their own. They would gladly pay a ransom. She just hoped someone heard her scream.

"C'mon! The van's in the alley. Pick her up and let's go!"

Luna felt her feet lift up from the ground and the slide of beefy arms under her knees and armpits. Should she struggle? She tried to wiggle free, but the arms around her tightened. They walked a few steps and then turned into a shadowy alley. Oh God, this was actually happening. Or maybe it was a mistake. Maybe they were trying to kidnap someone else.

"Get her in the van and tell her to stop—*What the fuck?*"

Something made the man who was carrying her freeze and suddenly, the air grew thick. The snowfall had picked up now, raining thick flakes down on them.

"*Motherfucker*...what is that thing?"

Luna was facing away from the street and she tried to turn her head to see what was going on. She couldn't see anything, but she heard clicks of something sharp on the pavement and a loud growl, like that coming from an animal. A very large animal.

A guttural cry pierced the still air, and Luna abruptly found herself on the ground, making her cry out in pain. The man who had been carrying her had dropped her unceremoniously. As she rolled to her hands and knees, she shook her head, trying to unscramble her brain and figure out what was going on.

Luna lifted her head and blinked several times. There was a huge dog—no—a *wolf* in the alley, snarling and growling at one of the kidnappers, trapping him against the wall. One of them was huddled in the corner clutching his arm while the man who had been holding her approached the animal from behind and Luna saw something glinting in his hand. A gun.

"No!" Luna warned.

The wolf turned its head and seeing the gun, immediately jumped on the attacker, knocking him to the ground. Its massive paws held the man down and then the large, bared teeth chomped down on his shoulder.

"Let's get outta here!" The other man cried as he helped his colleague up.

Luna quickly scrambled against the wall, shrinking into the shadows and prayed that the kidnappers had forgotten about her. They must have because both men jumped into the van and backed it up.

She screamed. The rear of the van collided with the wolf, sending it back a couple of feet. The whine of pain sent a stab of worry through her and she ran to the wolf's side. Meanwhile, one of the kidnappers hopped out of the van and helped the third up, tossing him into the back of the vehicle.

Good riddance. She knelt down holding her breath as she carefully laid a hand on the injured animal. What kind of wolf was it? She'd seen these animals on TV, but they were never this massive. The head alone was the size of her torso and it must be over six feet tall sitting up.

She brushed the fur on the wolf's head aside, trying to figure out how bad it was hurt. When she stared down into its face, she gasped and drew her hand back. Turquoise eyes looked up at her. Familiar eyes.

Luna watched in horror as the head began to shrink. Midnight fur sank back into skin and its snout flattened back. Limbs shortened, claws retracted, and its canines receded into a smaller, very human mouth.

"No," she whispered. Her legs wouldn't move and her arms

stayed very still at her side. As the wolf transformed back into Killian, her breath caught in her throat.

"Luna," he rasped. "I...I can explain. Please, stay here."

Her mouth dropped open as she watched a very naked Killian get up, walk back into the shadows and come back, hopping into a pair of jeans.

"A-a-aren't you cold?" she asked with a blank stare. The snowflakes landing on his bare chest melted when they touched the hot skin.

"No, my kind doesn't get cold easily," he said as he took her elbow and helped her up. "Jesus, you're shaking. You must be in shock. Dammit!" he cursed when his eyes landed on the bruise on her cheek. "It's already healing. Good." He let out a frustrated sigh and ran his fingers through his hair.

"I want to go home, Killian," she said slowly. There was a buzzing in her ears, and she feared she might faint.

"Of course, I'm taking you home. To my home. But first, we need to stop uptown."

"What?" she asked incredulously, her head snapping up at him. "What happened? Oh my God, you're a...you..." Her throat was closing up and she couldn't make out the words..

"Yes, I'm a wolf. Or as we prefer to be called—Lycans. Now," Killian drew her coat tighter around her, "let's go flag a cab, and I'll explain everything."

"O...okay..."

She followed him meekly out of the alley to the street corner. The meager light under the lamppost highlighted his features, while adding shadow to others. He appeared at once familiar and alien, causing a shiver to ripple through her. "Explain. Now."

Killian took a deep breath. "I'm not sure where to begin, but here's the short version. Wolf shifters, like me, have existed for a long time without the larger human population knowing. We live like normal people except, well, we can turn into wolves. Lycans also have enhanced strength and senses."

Luna still couldn't believe it, but she had seen it with her own eyes. "Where are we going?"

"I have to take you to the Alpha. Most Lycans live in clans. It helps keep everyone safe and the secret easier hide. New York is just one of many clans around the world."

"Wait—so you're taking me to your leader?" Oh God, what would happen? Would they silence her?

"Grant Anderson is Alpha of New York and leader of this territory, but he's not my Alpha. I don't have one."

"I'm confused. What do you mean you don't have an Alpha?"

Killian's jaw tightened. "I'll explain more later, but I'm a Lone Wolf. It's a special status for Lycans like me who have no clan." He raised his hand to flag a passing cab and when the driver stopped in front of them, he opened the door. "Get in and you'll know more."

Luna considered running for a moment, but what would she do? Where would she go? With a loud gulp, she slid into the seat and Killian climbed in right after her.

"Upper West Side," he told the cabbie. "I'll let you know when we're there."

7

"When I let you stay in my territory, I was expecting you to behave," Grant Anderson said as he walked out into the living room of his plush penthouse apartment. The Alpha was dressed in a sleeping robe, his hair disheveled and he wore a scowl on his face. "Tell me I'm not going to regret my decision."

"Sorry for getting you up in the middle of the night, Alpha," Killian said with a curt bow. "This is Luna Rhoades," he introduced.

Grant eyed Luna, his eyes immediately drawn to her belly. Luna's cheeks turned pink. "How do you do?"

He nodded back but didn't approach her. "Ms. Rhoades," he acknowledged. "Please sit. Tell me, did you see Killian's wolf?" Straight to the point. Grant wasn't Alpha for nothing.

"Y-y-yes," she stammered. "It...he...saved me from these men who were trying to kidnap me."

"Dammnit, Killian, other people saw you in Lycan form?" Grant ran his palm down his face. "Nick will deal with that. Dr. Faulkner is on his way to examine Ms. Rhoades. But, you're sure she's your True Mate?"

"Yes, Alpha," Killian confirmed. "Meredith can attest to that."

"Congratulations." A petite woman stepped out from the same door Grant came from. Her thick, curly, dark hair flowed in waves down her shoulders, and her green silk robe was wrapped around a large, very pregnant belly.

"*Lupa*," Killian greeted the Alpha's wife. "Apologies for disturbing your sleep."

"We weren't sleeping," Frankie Anderson said in an amused voice that made Grant's scowl deepen.

"Then I should probably say sorry again," Killian replied.

"It's all good. Besides, I was curious." Frankie's mismatched blue and green eyes looked at Luna warmly. "Another one," she exclaimed, moving closer to Luna. "*Amazing*. May I?"

Luna looked up at the petite woman and nodded. Frankie sat next to her and placed her hand on her belly. "Good... strong..." she said. "Want to feel mine?" Luna nodded and Frankie took her hand and placed it on her bump. "One more month," Frankie said, rubbing her belly. "One more month and I get to see my baby."

The door to the suite opened making Luna jump in surprise. An older man wearing a trench coat and holding a medical bag strode in.

"I'm Dr. Tom Faulkner," he introduced. "You must be Ms. Rhoades. I'm the clan's official doctor, and I'd like to give you an initial examination. Is that all right?"

Luna nodded. "Of course."

"Let's go to the guest room," Frankie suggested. Dr. Faulkner helped Frankie and Luna up, and then the Lupa led them to the hallway on the other side of the room.

"Well, this is going to complicate things," Grant said as he walked to liquor cabinet in the corner of the room. He selected a decanter filled with amber liquid and poured two glasses. He handed one to Killian.

"Thanks," he said, accepting the glass. "It certainly is. I swear, Alpha, I didn't know she was still pregnant. She told me it was gone." He didn't want Grant to think Luna was capable of getting rid of a pup. Many Lycans were sensitive about that, especially with their dwindling numbers.

"She lied to you?"

"It was for the baby's sake," he assured Grant. "Look, that's not point. She's here and so is the baby. I'm going to raise the pup with her."

"As you should," Grant replied.

"And she already knows about us, so all we have to do is petition the Council and she can pledge to the Lycans."

"It sounds simple, but as you know, things with the Lycan High Council have been in chaos, ever since Rodrigo's treachery came out." Grant took a sip. "But, I'll see what I can do. We have to tell them about Luna, though they won't be happy about all these complications. They'll want to know where she's been, who she's told and if anyone else knows that she's carrying a True Mate child."

"What can they do anyway? If—"

"Killian! I got your text. Where is she? Is she all right?"

Meredith materialized out of thin air next to the planter in the corner of the living room with her husband, Daric, right beside her. He looked slightly annoyed, his blue-green eyes piercing right into Killian.

Grant groaned. "Call next time you plan to pop in, okay?"

"Sorry, Alpha," Daric huffed in apology. "But Meredith was quite insistent we had to be here now."

"My niece or nephew's baby mama was attacked!" Meredith exclaimed. "Of course we had to be here now. Did you kick their asses, Killian?"

"I hurt one of them, but they all got away."

"Fuck. I'm gonna murder them, then Daric will bring them back to life, then I'm gonna kill them again," Meredith said, her eyes glowing.

"I cannot bring the dead back to life, *min kjære*," Daric pointed out.

"Yeah, well I'm gonna make them bleed. No one hurts my family and gets away with it."

Grant heaved a heavy sigh. "Anyway, going back to the problem at hand. I think it would be best for Luna if she stayed here in the Enclave. She'll be protected, have round the clock security, and she'll be close to the Medical Wing."

"No," Killian growled. "She stays with me." The thought of being away from Luna was making his wolf antsy. She'd been away from them for too long.

"I know the feeling of not wanting to be away from your mate, Killian, especially at this time," Grant said, glancing to where Frankie had taken Dr. Faulkner and Luna. "But we can't have her loose around New York. She hasn't been properly vetted, and we can't be sure she won't talk to the press or the police."

"She won't," Killian assured Grant. "I know she won't. And I won't let her out of my sight."

"Why don't you let 'her' make that decision?" Luna said as she walked back into the living room. Her back was straight as a board and her face drawn into a scowl. "I'm not some child. I have my own place, a job, and life."

"You don't need to go back to that place," Killian declared. "I have lots of space and my building is safe. And you never have to work again. I have plenty of money to support you and the baby. You're coming home with me."

"I'm going home to my apartment." Luna put her hands up and stalked over to Killian. She poked his chest. "I'm not taking your money. I know where it came from. Do they know that you're a thief and liar? That you steal things and sell them for money?"

Killian was silent, but Meredith guffawed. "Yeah, we all do," she said wryly. "I mean, we did. Me, Killian, Connor, and Quinn. But we're legit now. Mostly."

Luna looked at them like they were all insane. "I'm going home."

"My dear," Dr. Faulkner said, putting a reassuring hand on her shoulder. "As I said, my initial examination of you isn't enough. You must come to the Medical Wing first thing tomorrow for more tests."

"Which is why she'll stay here with us," Frankie insisted.

"The hell she will!" Killian shouted.

"Killian, don't yell at my wife," Grant warned, the air around them suddenly growing thick.

Killian gave Frankie a nod. "Apologies, Lupa, I mean no disrespect. But you understand, right? She should be with her mate."

Frankie's blue and green eyes turned to steel. "You may be the father of her child," she said in an icy voice. "But whether you're her mate is still debatable. A mate wouldn't let the mother of his pups get to this state."

Grant walked over to his wife and put an arm around her shoulder. "It's all right, sweetheart."

"Look at her!" Frankie exclaimed, her body shaking. "She's not healthy. She's practically starving."

Frankie's piercing gaze and cutting words made guilt slash through Killian. The Lupa was right, of course. She nailed it.

"He didn't know," Luna spoke up. "I...I hid the baby from him."

Killian's head jerked towards her. Why was Luna defending him? She had Frankie Anderson, Lupa of New York and Alpha of New Jersey on her side. She could have Killian tossed out on his ass or worse, yet she chose to make excuses for him. Maybe all hope wasn't lost and Luna still cared for him.

"Please, Alpha," Killian said. "Let me take her home. She'll be safe with me."

"I already said I'm going home."

"You can't let her go."

"She'll be okay in the guest room. I'll make sure she's okay until the baby is born."

Everyone was talking at the same time until finally, Meredith put her fingers to her lips and whistled.

"All right, all right, everyone just pipe down!" Meredith put her hands on her hips. "You," she said to Killian. "You don't have the right to tell her what to do just because you knocked her up. And you," she turned to Grant. "You can't keep her a prisoner here. Because that's what you're trying to do, right? Want to put a tracking bracelet on her too?"

"Are you telling your Alpha what to do?" Grant asked incredulously.

"I'm not done!" Meredith held up her hand. "Lupa," she said to Frankie. "Thank you for your generous offer, but I think it would be best if Luna were somewhere safe, where she can feel more normal and at home."

"And that would be?"

"Why, with me of course!" Meredith said cheerfully. "Where else? We're practically family."

"No way. She's coming home with me," Killian argued.

"I think staying with Meredith makes perfect sense," Frankie nodded in agreement. "You can bring her back here for her full examination tomorrow."

"I can protect her," Killian interjected. "She'll be safe with me."

"Oh please, Killian," Meredith said. "Where could she possibly be safer than with two Lycans, a warlock, and dragon?"

"A what and what?" Luna asked, her eyes darting back and forth between Meredith and Killian.

"I'll explain later," Meredith said, patting her head. "It's settled then. Daric, let's go. Bye everyone, see you in the morning!"

Meredith grabbed Luna's arm and they disappeared before anyone could protest.

"Fucking Meredith," Killian and Grant said at the same time.

Dr. Faulkner looked amused and Frankie laughed. "Good luck to you," she said to Killian. "But trust me," she added, patting her belly and giving Grant a warm look. "It's all worth it."

Luna heaved a gasp as the coldness that gripped her body slowly ebbed away. She blinked a couple of times and then opened her eyes. She was standing in the middle of a cavernous living room, decorated lushly in warm shades of olive, blue and brown. A large leather sectional sofa was in one corner in front of a sixty inch HDTV screen. There was also a ten foot tall stuffed unicorn with a golden horn in the corner, grinning at her. Where was she?

"Welcome home," Meredith said. "Our home, I mean."

"I hope you'll be comfortable," the man standing next to her said. He had been at the penthouse but didn't speak. The man was tall and handsome, with long blonde hair tied back in a ponytail. Eyes like the clear ocean looked back at her. "I'm Daric."

"He's my baby daddy," Meredith said proudly.

"Husband," Daric corrected.

"Aww, of course, honey. You're my number one." She gave his butt a playful squeeze, and he rolled his eyes then smiled warmly at her.

Luna watched them, pushing the envy deep down. Not that she begrudged Meredith and Daric, but she knew a loving relationship like theirs was something she would never have.

"So, Luna, are you hungry?" Meredith's eyes lit up. "What am I saying, of course, you are. You both are," she laughed, looking at her belly.

She blushed. Frankie had mentioned something about having an unusual appetite when they were pregnant with... what did she say? Something about a mate. The kindly old doctor commented that she was underweight for someone in her state, to which she'd blurted out that she just didn't have a lot of money for extra food. Frankie had looked livid and Luna was scared that the other woman would give birth right then and there. She didn't tell her why she was broke, but Frankie was smart enough to figure it out on her own.

Truthfully, she should have been more resistant. Werewolves were real. They were living right under everyone's noses and everyone she met tonight was one, except for Meredith's husband. But he had magical powers. What else was real? Werebears? Mermaids? Her mind was reeling with the possibilities. Lycans were real, and she was carrying one of them.

Meredith had led her to the kitchen, made her sit on one of the stools around the counter, and proceeded to take out various plastic containers. "Don't worry, we'll get you healthy soon enough."

"You don't have to do this." But Luna's eyes grew wide when Meredith began to lay out the food. Bread, cold cuts, pastries, pasta, half of a roasted chicken, some ham. Her stomach grumbled loudly and she blushed.

"You don't have to be embarrassed," Daric soothed. "We're all used to pregnant mates and their appetites."

"Thank you for letting me stay," she replied. Luna didn't want to impose, but after her kidnapping attempt, she was scared of being alone.

"It's the right thing to do," he stated. "And it makes Meredith happy."

"And you don't have to stay up with me for my two a.m. feedings," Meredith said wryly.

She handed Luna a croissant and she eagerly took it, taking a huge bite. "Oh my God, this is amazing! Reminds me of the croissants I had when I went to this conference in Paris."

"We brought them back a few days ago," Meredith said. "Daric can pick you up some freshly-baked ones in the morning."

"Er...that's okay," Luna stammered. Right. Daric apparently had the ability to travel halfway across the world in a second. "This is still good." She finished the whole thing and then accepted a loaded plate from Meredith.

"I'll leave you girls to your feast," Daric said. He leaned down and kissed Meredith on the cheek then walked towards the steps that led up to a lofted bedroom.

"I just texted Jade. That's my best friend and neighbor. She's hungry, too and will be right up," Meredith said through a mouthful of apple pie. "Oh, I hear the front door. That's her. Don't worry, you'll love Jade. She's sweet."

A few moments later, a petite brunette walked into the loft. She was pretty, with long brown hair that was tied back in a messy braid. As she approached them, she let out a sleepy yawn and rubbed her pregnant belly.

"Oh wow, is everyone around here pregnant?" Luna belatedly slapped her hand over her mouth. It was rude of her, but she couldn't help it. Who the heck wasn't knocked up?

The brunette laughed and held out her hand. "I'm Jade. Jade Cross." Jade had a soft, posh voice with a slight English accent. Up close, she was even prettier, with her light green eyes and creamy rosy skin.

"Luna Rhoades," she replied, shaking the other woman's hand.

"How far along are you?" Jade asked as she sat down next to Meredith and began to pile her plate with food.

"Um, about four months? I'm not sure. I haven't been to a doctor."

"Well, when was the first time you and Killian had sex?"

Jade gave her friend a warning look and Luna bit her lip as her eyes dropped to the floor.

Meredith rolled her eyes. "Oh, c'mon. I don't want to hear the details. Eww, gross. But if you can narrow it down then you can figure out the due date. I'm sure Dr. Faulkner will ask you tomorrow."

"Did he ask you?" Jade inquired.

"No, but I told him anyway," Meredith said.

"Er..." Luna's brows knitted.

"Oh, sorry," Meredith sighed. "I forgot you don't know anything about True Mates, yet. Let me give you the rundown."

"I'm a doctor," Jade said. "I should explain it to her."

"Well, I tell it better. Here," she shoved an egg tart in the pretty Lycan's mouth. "We just got these in Hong Kong. They're still warm."

Jade tried to protest through a mouthful of pastry, but Meredith shushed her. "So, where do I begin? Lycans, as you know, exist. We have wolves living inside of us and sometimes we let them out to have a little bit of fun. Don't worry, we're all in full control of our wolves and sworn to secrecy, never to reveal ourselves to the general public."

"Right," Luna said. She got that part.

"Lycans also have an infertility problem. Not, you know," she made a gesture with her index finger, crooking it down and whistling a sad tune. "Trust me. Or I'm sure you know, am I right?"

Luna blushed. No, Killian never had problems performing in the bedroom. If anything, he was always in the mood.

"Get on with it," Jade grumbled as she swallowed the last bit of egg custard.

"Yes, yes," Meredith said rolling her eyes. "See, Lycans can't always have kids. It's very hard for couples to conceive and those who do rarely have more than one. Also, if a Lycan were to mate with a human, they always have a human kid. Now, apparently, one exception is the True Mates. True Mates always conceive the first time they boink without condoms. Even if you're on birth control."

"So why don't Lycans just have kids with their True Mates?" Luna asked.

"Well, no one really knows how to find their True Mates," Meredith replied. "You just kind of find each other."

"And there weren't a lot of those types of pairing. Until now," Jade said, rubbing her belly.

"Yeah, after like, a million years—"

"Decades," Jade corrected.

"Right. True Mate pairings weren't common. In fact, no one's had a True Mate for at least a generation. Until about…oh, over a year ago? That's when it started. Since then, True Mate pairings have been popping up. Like Daric and me."

There was a lot of information processing in her head, but Luna tried to keep up. "So, wait. Daric's not a human or Lycan, though, right?"

Meredith shook her head. "Nuh-uh. He's a warlock."

"They exist, too?"

"Yup. Warlocks and witches, though they don't usually like us much."

"Are there other creatures like you? I mean—werebears? Werelions? How about vampires?"

Meredith chortled. "No. No. And eww, no."

"So just wolves, huh?"

"And dragons. Well, one dragon," Jade said. "My mate is a dragon, but Sebastian's one of a kind. It's a long story. I'll tell you about it some other time."

"Right." Wolves and Dragons—check. She took a piece of chicken breast and stuffed it into her mouth, contemplating everything she had heard.

"Don't worry, Luna, it'll all be okay," Meredith assured her. "Your baby will be fine. Remember what I told you? We're invincible. We can get stabbed, shot, poisoned..."

"Thrown off a cliff," Jade reminded her.

"Oh yeah, that was a good one," Meredith chuckled. "Anyway, nothing can harm you or the baby while you're pregnant."

Luna gasped. "I was in an accident the other day. A hit and run."

"Yeah, good thing you were preggers then," Meredith said. "Of course, the downside is that sonograms don't work on us. We don't know the sex of the baby until they're born." She rubbed her belly. "I've been praying for a girl. I saw the cutest Ariel onesie the other day, and I bought it. I've been keeping it from Daric because I think he knows it'll be a boy," she pouted.

"Well, I'm glad to know that," Luna said, managing a smile.

"So, can I ask you something?" Meredith said in a small voice.

"Sure."

"About Killian."

"Oh." Her hand trembled, and she nearly dropped the glass she was holding. "Um..."

"I don't want to be nosy..." Jade guffawed and Meredith elbowed her. "But...I think Killian is still in love with you. Do you love him?"

Luna went quiet. Did she ever love him? Or was what she felt because they were somehow thrown together by magic, fate, biology, or whatever was behind True Mates?

"Killian hasn't been the same since he came to New York. When our dad died, he was devastated of course, we all were. But it's been months, and he hasn't even shown any signs of being his old self. And now I know that's because of you."

"Wait. Your dad died?" Guilt and sadness washed over her. Killian. Who was with him when his father died? Did someone help him through the grief? No, she shouldn't think of such things. She hated him. But a small, unacknowledged part of her was aching for him.

"Our adoptive father. Archie took Killian, Quinn, Connor, and me in when we were orphaned. Anyway," Meredith continued. "I know he hurt you and left you to fend for yourself. But he's a good guy and we could always count on him to do the right thing. He's our big brother, our leader, and he's always put everyone's interests ahead of his own." Meredith looked at Luna with pleading eyes. "I think...if you give him a chance, he can be a good mate and a good father."

"Why are you telling me this?" she asked defensively.

"Because I miss the old Killian," Meredith murmured. "The one who used to make me laugh. Who could charm the pants off anyone and didn't take things so seriously. I miss that light in his eyes."

Luna didn't know what to say. Killian did seem different. She knew what Meredith was talking about though. He used to have this mischievous sparkle in his eyes that could make anyone smile. "I don't know, Meredith. I need time."

"Think about it, will you? Because something tells me, he's not going to let you go easy."

She placed a hand on her stomach. "You mean, our baby." Maybe that's what he really wanted. His Lycan child.

Meredith let out a sigh. "Think what you like, but he may surprise you."

Luna pushed her empty plate away from her, finally full. "Thank you for the meal."

"You can have anything you want in the house, okay? Don't worry, we have plenty more. Now, let me show you to your room. We're still renovating and haven't figured out the final layout, so don't worry if you wake up and there's a wall somewhere that didn't have one before. It's perfectly normal."

Somehow, Luna knew that her definition of perfectly normal was about to change.

8

The storm had slowed down considerably, though the ground was already blanketed in snow. Killian leaned against the wall, looking up at the building across the street, watching the lights go on and off through the windows.

As soon as Meredith, Daric, and Luna disappeared, Killian left the Enclave. He told Grant that he was going home, but somehow he found himself outside the converted warehouse loft where Meredith and Daric lived.

His inner wolf was restless. It wouldn't stop hounding and scratching at him, urging him to try and get as close as possible to Luna. *This is as close as we get, buddy,* he said to the antsy wolf, but it wouldn't listen. It needed to know she and the pup were okay.

With an impatient sigh, he crossed the street to the building. Meredith and Daric didn't have a security system in place which made his life easier. Picking their lock and getting in was the simple part. As he crept into the living room, he sighed in relief as he saw the layout hadn't changed much since the last time he was here. He walked across the loft to the hallway on the right which led to the set of bedrooms. Luna's delicious scent lingered in the air, and he only had to follow his nose to know which bedroom she was sleeping.

Killian supposed it was apt that moonlight streamed straight down from the skylight and onto the bed, illuminating the woman who had been occupying his mind for the better part of the last four months. She faced him, her features calm in repose as she slept on her side. She was wearing a sheer cotton nightgown and he could make out a nipple poking through the fabric. Desire surged back to him, but he wasn't sure if it was ever really gone.

"Are you just going to stand there?" she asked, her eyes staying closed.

"How did you know I was here?"

"I can smell your cologne," she sighed as her lids opened. "What time is it?"

"Just after two."

She sat up slowly and Killian couldn't help but follow the line of her body. Her breasts seemed lusher and made his cock stand to attention. When his gaze landed on her swollen belly though, pride and something primal filled him. He stifled a groan, his emotions churning. At this moment, Luna carrying his child was the only thing that made sense in the world.

"It feels like it's been a million years since I left the restaurant," she said. She swung her legs over the side of the bed. "What are you doing here?"

"I needed to see you. To make sure you're okay."

"As you can see, I'm all right," she stated. "Now, please go."

He nodded and turned to leave, but when Luna's face twisted and her hand dropped to her belly, he suddenly found himself sitting next to her on the bed. "What's wrong? Are you okay? Is it the baby? Should we call the doctor?"

"No, don't bother Dr. Faulkner. It's just..." She looked up at him. "The baby is awake."

His eyes glazed over as he looked at her belly and his breath caught in his throat.

"Do...do you want to touch?" she asked, her voice hesitant. "I'm not sure how much you can feel. He or she is only about the size of a lemon."

Killian desperately wanted to but knew he had to tread carefully. "Only if you want me to."

There was a pause, but she nodded, her short, shiny locks bobbing against her chin. He wavered for a second before placing a large hand on her belly. As soon as he made contact with the bump, he felt a small surge of power. His eyes widened and a lump got stuck in his throat.

When he opened his mouth to speak, it was only then he realized he had stopped breathing. He put both hands on her belly, trying his hardest not to lean down and lay his cheek against her.

"I'm sorry about your father. Meredith told me he died."

Killian froze. He thought he had lost two people that day—Archie and this child. He searched within himself, trying to find that anger at Luna he had held on to all these months, but it just wasn't there.

"I'm sad Archie's not going to be here for this," he answered, rubbing her stomach.

"He knew?"

"Yes, he was the only person I told." He took a deep breath and withdrew his hands. "He was excited about being a grandfather."

"But he wasn't your real dad?" Luna asked.

"No. Archie adopted all of us, but not at the same time. I was the first." He looked to the large window on the far side of the room, watching the tiny snowflakes drifting across the glass. "When I was six years old, my entire clan was murdered and we —the children—were taken away. Another group of Lycans were going to train us to become compliant soldiers for their cause." He paused at Luna's soft gasp before continuing. "I was in their facility for a year. All the children were separated, made to stay in single rooms. I don't remember a lot from that time except being bored and hearing other kids cry. Sometimes, I would cry too." A small, warm hand wrapped around his. "It was a year later that Archie found me. He broke into the facility which was easy for him being a master thief and all. He took me and brought me home."

"What happened to the other children?" Luna's voice creaked as if she was afraid to know the answer.

"He tried to go back for the other kids, but when he got back to the facility, it was gone. Burned to the ground."

Luna let out a soft cry and wrapped her arms around herself.

"Archie told me he kept trying to find them, but he never did. It's a long story, but basically, there were some bad Lycans allied with our enemies who were trying to build an army to take over both Lycan and human society. Archie kept the files on all of us and I read mine, including some of his notes. He thinks that it was too risky to kidnap the children outright and keep them so instead, those traitors did what they could to ensure that more and more Lycans were torn apart from their clans to force them to become Lone Wolves like us. They kept track of those Lone Wolves and a few months ago, made them fight in their war."

"Meredith? Your other brothers? Archie took them in, too?"

He nodded. "Yes. They have their stories to tell and I don't know all the details. But, Archie found us and saved us."

"He sounds like a good man. A good father," Luna said.

"Yes, he was." He looked down at her, sensing her fear and hesitation. "Those traitors are gone now. We defeated them and they won't be back. No one will ever hurt you or our child."

Luna said nothing but swallowed visibly. She crept back into bed and under the covers. "If you want to...you can stay. Looks like the storm's picking up again."

Outside, the wind was blowing the snow sideways and the windows rattled. "I'll sit over there," Killian said, walking over to the easy chair in the corner. By the time he sat down, Luna was fast asleep, her breathing even and steady. She was so achingly beautiful and Killian felt regret creeping in.

Moving to New York seemed like a good idea at the time because he knew that even if she had aborted their baby, he wouldn't have had the strength to stay away from her. He would have crawled back, asked her to forgive him for leaving her holding the bag; would have done whatever it took to make her his again. His need to be with her all this time and the hatred he had felt for her was an internal battle he'd been struggling with for months. Now, he couldn't find a reason to hate her anymore —but she still loathed him for destroying her life. He had to find a way to make it up to her.

The chair was much too small for him and no matter what position he curled into, there was no way he was going to get any sleep. Glancing over to the large bed Luna occupied, he told himself there was lots of space. She was curled up in one corner. He could lie down beside her and never touch her. Besides, they had shared a bed before. He pushed those thoughts away quickly since most of those times never involved sleeping. Decision made, he stood up and padded over to the bed, removed his shoes, socks, and pants, and then lay on top of the covers as far away from Luna as possible.

The smell of fresh rain in the morning wrapped around Luna and for a moment she thought she was stuck in some dream of the past. But no, she was definitely awake in the present, and the heavy arm over her waist was very real.

Luna held her breath. Her back was pressed against a very hard, masculine chest. Memories of last night came back into her foggy brain, and she realized it was Killian's muscled arm draped over her waist, his large hand spanning her belly. Glancing down, she recognized the wolf's head tattoo on his forearm. She remembered how much she loved tracing her fingers over the ink, but never had the courage the ask him what it meant. Now she could guess.

The weight of his arm was uncomfortable and she couldn't breathe, so she shifted, lifting her torso up so she could move his arm away. However, this only gave him an opportunity to slide his other arm underneath her, his arms wrapping around her and his hand landing on her breast.

Her nipples instantly puckered and wetness pooled between her legs. Luna had heard that pregnancy hormones made women horny, but she supposed that with being exhausted—first from the trial, then moving to New York, she hadn't had time to think about sex. But now here she was, wrapped up in the arms of the man she was supposed to hate and all she could think about was how long it had been since she'd last had an orgasm.

And maybe it wasn't just her thinking about sex. Something very hard was pushing against her ass. She pressed back which made him groan sleepily and nuzzle her neck. Oh God, that almost made her cream her panties. Killian knew how much she loved having her neck kissed and it was like he was torturing her on purpose.

"Kill..." she moaned softly. Really, she meant to make that sound more irritated, but it came out like she was in heat. Oh dear, he was grinding against her ass now, and his hand began to knead her breast. She bit her lip. She was afraid of waking Killian, but she wasn't sure whether it was because he would stop or if he would take this further.

"Luna," he murmured against her shoulder. "So good..."

Damn pregnancy hormones were going into overdrive. *Oh, fuck it.* Not like she'd ever get another chance to get off again. She grabbed her borrowed nightgown (saying a silent sorry to Meredith) and raised it up over her waist so she could feel him. Killian shifted his hips to push his underwear down and a very hard and very naked cock pressed up against her back.

"Oh..." she moaned as his hand snaked down between her legs. The rough pads of his fingers worked along her already wet slit, teasing her before parting the nether lips to slip inside.

"*Killian.* I—" She turned her head to look back at him and he moved his mouth over hers. The first touch of their lips sent shock straight down to her core, igniting something she thought was gone. As his fingers plunged into her pussy, she felt the edges of a white heat slowly spreading through her body. She moved against him, bumping forward to meet his fingers as her ass cheeks pressed back onto his cock. Pre-cum leaked from the tip of his cock, smearing her backside.

He released her mouth, his lips going for the soft spot behind her ear. She moaned aloud, feeling his teeth scraping the skin. His hand found her breast, tweaking her sensitive nipples through the cotton fabric.

"Killian!" she mewled as her orgasm hit her fast and he plunged three fingers deep inside her. She moved against him and he let out a groan as thick spurts of his seed painted her back. God, it was so hot, and her body was buzzing with excitement. Sex with Killian was the best she ever had, that was for sure.

His ragged breathing turned even and she felt a soft cloth rubbing on her. Turning back, she saw Killian had taken his shirt off and was wiping her clean. He tossed the shirt aside when he was done and then slipped back into bed, cuddling her from behind.

"Why did...what did...?" She wasn't sure what to say. Was he just going to spoon her as if nothing had happened?

"I could smell how aroused you were."

"Smell how..." Oh right. Lycans. Oh crap, did he always smell her?

"I can smell when you're wet and when you're horny," he said in a teasing voice.

"You can not," she countered, turning around to face him.

"Oh yes, I can. In fact, you're still horny now. Want another orgasm?"

She grabbed a pillow and hit him over the head, but he only chuckled and tossed it to the floor. "Is that a yes?"

"Killian..." she warned in a serious voice. "We can't do this." She wanted him, that was for certain. Sex was never a problem between them. But there were too many things going on right now. She pulled away from him, trying to put some space between them.

He took her hand. "Move in with me. Today."

God, he was stubborn. "I can't."

"What do you mean, 'you can't'?" he asked. "Your place is with me. In my home and my bed. I think we just proved that."

Anger bubbled inside her and she rose from the bed. "We didn't prove anything."

"You still want me," he said smugly as his eyes dropped to her puckered nipples. "You want me right now."

The look on his face made her want to smother him with a pillow. "Get out."

"Only if you come with me. To my place."

She let out a frustrated groan. God, the man was stubborn. "Didn't you hear me? I have a life and an apartment and job—"

"And I said you never have to work again for the rest of your life. You're the mother of my child, and I'll be damned if you go back to that place or work at that restaurant." Killian rolled off the bed and stood up, towering over her, his arms crossed over his chest.

Luna's face flushed with anger and her hands drew into tight fists at her sides. "You can't tell me what to do!"

"Hey lovebirds, knock it off!" Meredith's voice rang through from the other side of the door. Before either of them could say anything, she barged in. "Jeez Louise, are you guys boinking or fighting? Either way, keep it down will ya!"

"Sorry," Killian grumbled.

"It's all right, we're awake anyway," she shrugged. "Breakfast should be here in five minutes. Come to the kitchen when you're done whatever it is you're doing."

Luna blushed and Killian smiled smugly.

"And for God's sake, Killian, put your dick away." Meredith gagged and slapped her palm over her eyes. "No one wants to see that shit. Except maybe Luna."

As the other woman walked out, Luna felt her face get even redder. It had been ages since she had last seen Killian naked. She'd forgotten how utterly delicious he was. His broad chest was muscled, and she noticed that he had a new tattoo on his shoulder, another wolf's head. A sprinkling of dark hair went all the way down, marking a happy trail that crossed over his defined six-pack. His cock, which was already semi-erect, was thick and long. As he bent down to pick up his discarded jeans,

Luna's eyes remained glued to his taut backside, the muscles rippling with every movement.

"So, you *do* like my dick, huh?"

Bastard. Luna turned around to hide her embarrassment, stomping over to the closet to grab one of the robes hanging inside. Wrapping the thick fabric around herself, she hoped it was enough to stop him from smelling how horny she was. *Fucking hell.* Mustering up her courage, she stalked back to him. "What happened this morning cannot happen again."

He crossed his arms over his chest and stared down at her with an amused look on his face. "Oh really?"

"Really. And I'm not moving in with you." There. She said it.

"We'll see about that, sweetheart."

Ugh, stupid man.

9

Things were tense between Killian and her when they left the guestroom, but Luna temporarily forgot why she was mad when the smell of food wafted into her nose.

Meredith and Daric had prepared a feast and the large kitchen island was heaped with food. There was a big dish of scrambled eggs, waffles, French toast, sausages, bacon, beans, fried mushrooms, a carafe of fresh orange juice, and a large pot of coffee. Her stomach gurgled hungrily, but no one made a comment though Daric smiled when he passed her a plate.

"Eat up," Meredith said, her plate already piled high. "Don't worry, there's enough for all of us."

Much to her annoyance, Killian took the plate from her hand and began to put some eggs on it. "I can do it myself," she said, trying to make a grab for the plate.

"Sit," he replied, pointing to the empty stool next to him. She pouted but sat down anyway. When he was satisfied with the amount of food on her plate, he placed it in front of her.

She would have protested more, but she was hungry. She dug in, putting a forkful of eggs into her mouth. It was so good; creamy and fluffy and seasoned just right. A moan escaped her throat which made Killian shoot her a heated look. Her cheeks flushed and she quickly swallowed her food, washing it down with orange juice.

"Good stuff?" Meredith asked with a raised brow.

"Yeah, thanks."

"Sounded like it."

She blushed even harder, wondering if Meredith's enhanced hearing had heard what happened that morning in the guest room. Oh God, how embarrassing. This wouldn't do. As much as it was nice to sleep in this luxurious apartment, she shouldn't get used to it. But what was she supposed to do now? Killian knew about the baby. He was right about one thing. It wasn't right to keep him away. Plus, what did she know about raising a Lycan? Would it transform right away and turn into a wolf? What would she do if her child attacked someone? And, there was someone out to get her. One of the reasons she didn't protest when Meredith took her home was she was scared. Those men from last night meant to kidnap her. Who were they?

"Stop worrying, sweetheart," Killian said, intruding on her thoughts. "I'll take care of you from now on."

"I'm not moving in with you," she said, sounding miffed.

"Uh-huh," he said absentmindedly, taking a bite of his waffles. "Meredith, I need to go to the office and sort out a couple of things. Will you take Luna to the Enclave for her appointment, please?"

"Of course," Meredith replied. "I need to see Dr. Faulkner, too."

"Is everything all right?" Daric asked, his face drawn into a frown.

"It's all fine, just a routine checkup," she assured her husband. "Luna, you're about Jade's size. She dropped off a couple things you can borrow for now. We don't have time to swing by your place. Dr. Faulkner's expecting us in an hour so we'll cab it there, okay?"

She shrugged. "That's fine. I don't work at the gallery today, but I have the dinner shift at the restaurant."

Killian frowned, but said nothing and kept eating.

Once they finished breakfast and the dishes were put away, Luna went back to the guest room with her borrowed clothes, showered, and got ready for the day. As soon as she came out of the bathroom, Killian was waiting for her. He grabbed her by the waist, bent down and planted a hard kiss on her mouth, leaving her breathless when he finally pulled away.

"See you later, sweetheart," he said with a charming smile before he walked out of the room.

"Huh? See you...what?" Luna blinked several times, trying to get out of her daze. She braced herself against the wall, her knees refusing to solidify from their jelly-like state.

"Luna, honey, ya ready?" Meredith called out.

"Coming!" she said, grabbing her coat and walking out to the main living room.

She and Meredith grabbed a passing cab outside. Luckily, the streets of Manhattan had already been cleared of the snow and they made good time going to the Enclave.

"So, is the Enclave like the Lycan headquarters?" she asked as they approached the complex of buildings on the Upper West Side of Manhattan.

"Something like that," Meredith said. "The Alpha and Lupa live here, as well as the Beta—that's the second-in-command—and his family, plus most of the two hundred or so Lycans in the city. There's apparently some sort of magic spell around the place that makes humans ignore it," she explained. "It's like a mini-city and the medical wing is there, too. Of course, there's the Fenrir Corporation headquarters."

Luna wrinkled her nose. "Fenrir? That's the big conglomerate, right?" From what she could recall, Fenrir was in everything from manufacturing to construction.

"Oh yeah, Grant Anderson is CEO of Fenrir."

"Wow, Lycans really are everywhere," Luna remarked.

Meredith said nothing as they entered one of the buildings in the complex. The other woman seemed to know her way, so Luna followed her until they reached the medical wing. A nurse in a white uniform led Luna to an examination room where Dr. Faulkner was already waiting. The doctor asked her some standard questions, as well as some non-standard ones (though she'd never been to a prenatal exam, she was pretty sure no other doctor had asked her what types of injuries she'd survived.) He took a vial of her blood and other samples, gave her some advice and asked her to come back. Mostly though, he advised her to eat more and try to gain a few pounds. Easier said than done, but if she kept hanging around Meredith, she had a feeling that wouldn't be too difficult.

"My turn," Meredith said as Luna exited the room. "Wait for me, okay? Then we can go hang out and get some lunch or something."

"Sure." Where would she go, anyway? Would the Lycans let her leave? Looking around the waiting room, she contemplated her future. This baby was the most important thing in the world right now, and she supposed she could swallow her pride and accept something from Killian. Food expenses. Transport to prenatal appointments. Medical expenses. Did Lycans have insurance?

A ringing sound from her purse jarred her out of her thoughts. Her phone! It was one of those old flip phones that didn't have a lot of features, but she could call and text. Plus, the battery life on the thing was phenomenal.

"Hello?" she answered without checking the number.

"Luna, hey." It was Artie from the Tisch Gallery where she worked.

"Hey, Artie, what's up? I'm not scheduled today, am I?" She was pretty sure she wasn't supposed to be in today, but maybe she got her dates wrong.

"No, it's not that. Listen," Artie paused. "I got a strange phone call a couple minutes ago. Some guy called and he said you were quitting."

"What?" Luna shot to her feet, ignoring the strange look the nurse gave her. "Who?"

"Er, he said he was your boyfriend. The father of your baby."

Killian! Damn him. How did he find out which gallery she worked? "No, that's not right."

"So you're not quitting?"

How dare he? "No, I'm not. It must have been a prank call… or something."

Artie breathed a sigh of relief. "Great, because I don't wanna have to get someone new."

"Of course. I'll see you tomorrow." She hung up and tossed her phone into her purse. "*Goddammit.*" She was so angry, she kicked the couch. "That piece of shit."

"Ready, Luna?" Meredith asked as she came into the waiting wrong. "Hey, what's wrong?"

"It's your asshole brother, that's what's wrong," Luna cursed. "He called the gallery where I work at and told them I was quitting!"

"He did? That asshat!" Meredith's nostrils flared, and she cracked her knuckles. "I swear, these men sometimes…"

"Good thing the gallery called me. And—*oh crap*—the restaurant!" If Killian found the gallery, then he surely knew about the Emerald Dragon by now. He might already be on the phone with Mrs. Tan. Her heart sank. Mrs. Tan always respected her employees and to that she was grateful. Hearing from someone else that she quit would definitely make the older woman lose respect for Luna.

"I have to go downtown," she insisted. "Now." She hoped it wasn't too late.

"Now? But we haven't had lunch."

"I'll get you some good Chinese food." *If I'm allowed back at Emerald Dragon.*

"Fine, let's go."

The tiny, older Asian woman peered up at Killian with a razor-sharp gaze. "You say you're Luna's boyfriend?"

Why did this old woman make Killian feel like he was a schoolboy in the principal's office? "Um, yes ma'am."

"Hmmm." Silence. "She didn't tell me the father was in the picture."

"I am. Now."

"Hmmm."

Killian shifted in his seat and cleared his throat. "Look, Mrs. Tan, I came here to hand in Luna's notice."

"Hmmm."

He tugged at the collar of his shirt. "Luna's getting far too pregnant to be working on her feet."

"I was working in this restaurant for every one of my pregnancies," she declared. "They had to drag me out when my water broke."

"Right. But since I'm here now, she doesn't need to wait tables anymore."

"Oh yeah? Why did she have to come work here in the first place, hmmm? Where were you then?"

Jesus Christ, how hard was it to quit around here? "Look, that's not important."

"Luna's a good girl," she declared.

"I know that."

"So why would I just let her go with some stranger? You come in here, telling me one of my employees is quitting and I should just let her go?"

The woman did have a point. But why was she so difficult? It's not like he walked in here and carried Luna off on his shoulders. Maybe he should have and he wouldn't be standing here like a prisoner in front of a firing squad.

The door to the restaurant flew open, sending the cold air inside.

"Mrs. Tan! Don't listen to him," Luna pleaded as she burst through the door, Meredith trailing behind her. "You!" She shot daggers at Killian. "How dare you!"

How the fuck did she know he was here? "Sweetheart," he greeted, standing up to put an arm around her.

She shrugged him off. "Don't 'sweetheart' me, you asshole!" Her eyes blazed, the color shifting into a darker amethyst. "Are you trying to get me fired from here, too?"

"Look, I told you, you don't need to work anymore. Whatever you want, you'll have it. I don't care what it costs."

"Why won't you listen to me, you stubborn man?"

"I'm stubborn?" Damn woman.

She let out a cry of frustration. "I'm so sorry for the confusion, Mrs. Tan," she said to her boss. "I most certainly am not quitting."

"I hate to lose such an excellent waitress," Mrs. Tan tsked. "Customers love her. I bet some of them won't be coming back when they find out she quit."

"Meredith," Killian said. "Make sure the office sends out for lunch here two times—" The old woman coughed and raised a brow. "Make that three times a week."

Meredith suppressed a smile. "Will do."

"Make sure you order the egg rolls and lo mein," Mrs. Tan instructed.

Luna's eyes nearly popped out of their sockets, and when she opened her mouth to speak, the crafty old woman raised a hand to silence her.

"Is this man really the father of your baby?"

"Er, yes," she answered.

Mrs. Tan looked at Killian. "You rich? You can provide for her?"

"Yes," he said without hesitation.

"Good," she nodded and then turned to Luna. "You're fired."

"What?" she asked, her voice pitching higher than normal. "Please, you can't fire me! I need this job."

Mrs. Tan took her hands. "No, you don't. You have a man to take care of you and the baby, right?"

"But...but..."

Killian gave Luna a smug smile. "Say goodbye, sweetheart." He tugged her arm, dragging her out of the Emerald Dragon.

"We have excellent packages for wedding banquets!" Mrs. Tan called after them. "I give you good price!"

Killian waved goodbye to the old woman and continued pulling her along for half a block until she pulled free.

"Did you just bargain for me for some egg rolls and lo mein?" Luna shouted at him, her hands stiff at her sides.

"Technically, honey, he got you *and* the lo mein," Meredith quipped.

"Sweetheart," Killian soothed. "Aren't pregnant women supposed to not get stressed?"

"I'm invincible, you ass," she retorted. "And I needed that job."

"You don't need any job," Killian insisted.

She let out another frustrated scream and put her hands up. "I'm going home."

"Good, let's get out of this cold." He grabbed her elbow.

"I hope you're taking me to my apartment. In the East Village."

"No, I'm not. You're going to my place."

"Are you going to toss me over your shoulder and take me there?" she dared.

He was sorely tempted but didn't press his luck.

"Killian," Meredith said, putting a hand on his arm. "Take a chill pill, okay? Good. Now, I'm gonna go home. You guys sort this out. Why don't you go somewhere with Luna and talk? And —I can't believe I'm saying this to you, but—have a real, adult conversation. Stop trying to bully your way into her life, okay?" She turned to Luna and gave her a hug. "You have my number. Call me for anything." She gave Killian a last warning look before she pivoted towards the subway entrance on the other side of the street.

Killian sighed. "Fine. I took a car today. I'll bring you to your place."

New York City covered in snow was probably one of the prettiest things Luna had ever seen, but sulking in the front seat of Killian's Jeep, she could hardly enjoy it. The nerve of this man thinking he could just swoop in and rescue her like she was some damsel in distress. True, she was about one late paycheck away from living on the streets, but she didn't like having to be saved, especially not by some boorish alpha male like Killian.

She looked over at him, and while she forced herself to frown when he smiled at her, her traitorous little heart did flip-flops. This was the old Killian. The one who could make her laugh with a corny joke or make her dizzy with one look. Right now though, the look that followed that smile sent tingles straight between her legs and her nipples tightened in anticipation. Their activities that morning flashed in her mind, and she licked her lips. God, that orgasm was incredible. It had been too long. The memory of Killian's lovemaking made her ache. She bit her lip to stop herself from moaning aloud. The Jeep suddenly stopped and when she opened her eyes to ask him if they were at her place, his turquoise eyes bored right into her.

"Stop looking at me like that," she snapped.

"Then stop thinking about sex," he answered back in an amused tone. "I can smell you. Are you wet right now?"

Oh fuck. Pregnancy hormones strike again. "I—"

Killian reached over and hauled her onto his lap, reclining his seat to make room for her. His large fingers dug into her hair, pulling her head down for a kiss. It was uncomfortable at first, but Killian made her straddle his lap, cradling her belly between them. She sighed and leaned down against his chest. His hands gripped her waist, moving and grinding her back and forth on his hard-on, which was now pressing up against her core.

"Fuck, baby," he said as he tore his mouth away from hers. "This morning was just a prelude. I need you now."

Glancing outside, she realized they were outside her building. "Let's go up to my place," she urged, unlocking the driver's side door. Her knees were shaking as she got out of the car. Killian slipped out, grabbing her ass and giving it a hard squeeze. She gave a yelp and bounded to the entrance of her building.

"I can't wait to be inside you again," he whispered into her ear as she fumbled with her keys to the front door. "We might not make it to your apartment this time."

"Stop...distracting me," she moaned as a hand cupped her breast.

She somehow managed to open the front door and sprinted towards the stairs, Killian hot on her heels.

"Don't run," he growled, grabbing her hand as she reached the top. Killian was two steps below her, so they were almost the same height.

Facing him, she flashed a sassy smile. "Or what?" She swore she saw his eyes glow and excitement zinged through her body. He smashed his lips against hers, pulling her off her feet and half-carrying her the rest of the way to her apartment.

"Killian," she moaned as he pressed her up against the door. To her surprise, the door swung open and they stumbled inside.

The desire that had been coursing through her suddenly fizzled out, replaced by cold fear. Luna's eyes scanned the inside of her place. The sheets on the futon had been ripped off and the small table was tipped on its side. Her laptop was smashed on the floor. The dishes lay broken all over the linoleum floor, and the hotplate had a hole in the middle. A soft cry escaped from her mouth and strong arms wrapped around her, dragging her outside.

"Luna," Killian soothed as she turned in his arms and pressed her cheek to his chest. She breathed in his scent, letting it calm her as her body began to shake. "I won't let anything happen to you," he promised. "I swear, I'm going to find out who's out to get you, okay?"

She nodded and let him lead her outside. He helped her into the backseat of the car and clicked the seatbelt into place. "I need to make a call, stay here," he instructed as he closed the door.

Luna wrapped her arms around her belly, taking deep breaths as she watched Killian. His back was to her, but she could see the tension in his body as he spoke on the phone. He ended the call, ran his palm down his face and took a breath. Then, he dialed another number. After a few minutes, he slipped the phone back into his pocket and walked back to the car.

"Shit," he slapped his palms on the wheel. "Sorry. I just got off the phone with my boss. I forgot to tell him I wanted some time off, and now he's sending me overseas."

"You're leaving?" While she was still annoyed at him for his antics, the thought of not being with him made an ache build in her heart.

"I'm sorry, sweetheart," he said, turning the key in the ignition. "Sebastian promised it wouldn't take long and he'll give me the time off I need after this. I called Meredith. You're staying with her until I get back."

"What about my apartment? Do we need to file a police report?"

He shook his head. "I'll take care of it."

Luna leaned back against the leather seat, wondering what 'take care of it' entailed.

10

Luna stayed with Meredith and Daric again for the second night in a row. Killian dropped her off at the loft, leaving her with a kiss that curled her toes and a promise that they would talk as soon as he got back. She had a sinking feeling that his definition of 'talk' was him giving orders again, but what could she do? The lock on her apartment was busted, and even if she reported it, she knew her landlord wouldn't be able to fix it right away. Besides, those men from last night obviously knew where she lived. Would they come back for her? What did they want? Should she go to the police?

Meredith and Daric assured her that she would be safe with them, but that didn't make the fear in the pit of her stomach disappear. She tossed and turned, trying to quiet her mind, but when she closed her eyes all she could see was those men who sought to kidnap her and the disheveled state of her apartment. Killian didn't say when he'd be coming back, but she hoped it was soon.

Her baby must have sensed her fear and tension, as it was awake again, kicking and stirring inside of her. "He'll be back, baby," she cooed, rubbing her belly. "Don't worry—everything's going to be all right."

Luna overslept, and she felt embarrassed when she saw Meredith was waiting for her in the living room, curled up in front of the TV.

"I have to go to Fenrir today," Meredith said. "I can't leave you here, but I can't bring you with me since you don't have the proper security clearances. Would you mind if I dropped you off at Lone Wolf for a couple of hours? Connor and Quinn will be there. You'll be in good hands."

"Um, okay," she shrugged. "I have to go into the gallery at three, though."

"One of them could take you there and I'll pick you up when you're done," Meredith assured her.

After she got dressed (in more of Jade's borrowed clothes, including a beautiful winter maternity coat), they left the loft and took a cab to Lone Wolf Security.

"Okay, you remember the office," Meredith said as she walked her to the door of the building. "I'll see you at the gallery at six."

"See you," she said, waving at the other woman as the waiting cab sped away. With a last glance at the street, she walked in the door and headed for the elevators.

Luna knocked on the door, and when no one answered, she let herself in. The lobby was empty. She heard the slamming of a door somewhere down the hallway followed by the sound of footsteps getting louder and louder.

"I didn't know he'd be here," a brunette mumbled to herself as stomped to the desk and plopped down on the chair. Her pretty face was drawn into a frown, but as she looked up at Luna, her face broke into a smile. "Oh," she said, her toffee-colored eyes lighting up. "You must be Luna. I'm Evie," she introduced, getting up and walking over to her. "Evie King."

"Luna Rhoades. Nice to meet you." Meredith had told her that their part-time admin assistant might be at the office so she didn't have to worry about the 'sausage fest' at Lone Wolf.

"Can I get you something? Some water? Juice? Snacks? I just stocked the pantry." She motioned to the couch. "Please, have a seat."

"I'm fine thank you, Evie, but I will sit down." Luna eased herself down on the couch which was very plush. "Sorry to be such a bother."

"Oh, you're no bother at all," Evie assured her. "Meredith called me ahead of time and told me about your schedule. Connor will take you to the gallery." She winced when a loud crash sounded from one of the offices down the hallway.

"Still, I hate imposing on anyone," Luna said, chewing her lip. She glanced at the hallway. She had met Quinn briefly the other day, but not Connor. What was Killian's other brother like?

She didn't have to wait long to find out.

A large shadow filled the hallway and a tall, imposing figure stood eerily still, his tattooed arms crossed over a massive chest. Her eyes traveled up to the handsome face that was marred by a deep scar that ran down over his right eye, and probably down his cheek too, though it was covered by a thick, ruddy beard. So this was Connor. The air seemed to grow thicker as he remained rooted to the spot, staring at her.

"Connor," Evie said in a chilly voice. "This is—"

"I know who she is." Connor's voice was gruff and dismissive as his eyes dropped to Luna's stomach. Without any other acknowledgment, he pivoted and turned to the door.

"Hey!" Evie called. "Where are you going?"

"Out."

"You said you'd take Luna to the gallery."

"Stop nagging me, woman," Connor growled at Evie. "I

already told you I'd do it and I will. I just have stuff to do right now."

The door slammed so loud behind him that Luna jumped.

"Sorry," Evie said, her eyes lowering to the ground. "If he's not back in time, I'll get Quinn to take you."

"I can go to the gallery myself," she insisted.

Evie's gaze trailed back to the door. "He'll be back."

Luna sighed and sank back into the chair. Connor obviously didn't want to babysit her and once again she felt like a big inconvenience. Her heart sank. The last thing she wanted was to be a burden. Not sure what else to do, she picked up a magazine on the coffee table and started to read through it.

By the time she checked the clock, it was past noon. Her stomach gurgled noisily, and she spied over at Evie who was busy typing away at the computer. Maybe the other woman was human and didn't hear her stomach. Good thing, but then she wasn't sure what to do about lunch.

There was a knock on the door and Evie frowned. She checked her phone and then stood up to open the door.

"Selena," she said to the person on the other side of the door. "I'm so sorry, I completely lost track of time. Give me a few minutes and we can get lunch. Would you mind if Luna tagged along?"

"No worries, Evie-girl," the redhead who breezed in assured her. "Hello," she greeted Luna. "I'm Selena, Evie's best friend. Oh, no, don't get up." Selena plopped down beside her.

Luna guessed Selena to be only an inch or two taller than her, but she had an aura about her that seemed to fill the room. She wasn't conventionally beautiful, but she was cute. Thick, unruly auburn curls bounced around her, reminding Luna of that animated movie with the Scottish princess.

Expressive blue-gray eyes blinked at her. "Are you a Lycan?"

"Uh, no. Human," she said. Was it rude to ask people 'what' they were? "Are you?"

Selena laughed and then snorted in an unladylike manner. "Hell, no. I'm an almost witch."

"What's an almost witch?" Luna asked and Evie let out a giggle.

"That means—"

"Yo, Luna!" came a loud voice from one of the offices down the hallway. "Come in here!"

She frowned. Who was calling her?

"I'm ordering in lunch. Come and look at the menu and tell me what you want!"

Luna braced herself against the sofa to stand up, but Selena put a hand on her arm to stop her. "Hey you rude fuck!" the redhead called out. "You're gonna let a pregnant lady stand up and walk to you? Don't you have legs?"

There was a sound of a chair slamming against a wall then heavy footsteps echoing from the hallway.

"Who the fuck—" Quinn stopped short when his eyes landed on Selena. "Are you?"

"I'm—"

But before Selena could answer, the front door slammed open. Luna thought for a moment that Connor had returned, but she was wrong. Three men barged in brandishing guns. One of them went straight to the couch and pointed his weapon at Luna's face while another one strode behind the counter to where Evie sat.

Quinn let out a low growl and sprang forward, knocking the third man who had stayed by the door to the ground.

"Uh-uh, pretty boy," one of them warned Quinn. He was by far the smallest of the trio but had a mean face that was drawn into an ugly scowl. "Get off my friend. Or do you want this pretty one's brains all over the wall?" He had a gun trained on

Evie's forehead. The brunette sat very still, a mask of fear blanketing her face.

"Shit," Quinn cursed as he brushed himself off. "Don't hurt her, asshole."

"Only if you don't cooperate," the short man said. Luna observed that he was probably their ringleader.

"What do you want?" Quinn asked through gritted teeth.

He looked over to Luna. "Ah, there she is. That's her."

Were these the same men from the other night? No, she didn't recognize any of their voices. Maybe whoever was trying to kidnap her had sent new guys. Killian did hurt one of them pretty good.

"Don't you dare touch her," Selena said, putting herself in front of Luna.

"Selena, no!" Luna cried and yanked the redhead down to the couch. She couldn't let an innocent get hurt because of her.

"No, Luna!" Quinn shouted, but that earned him a knock on the head with the butt of a gun. He turned to his attacker, reaching out to him.

"Stop," the ringleader commanded, pressing the gun harder against Evie's temple.

"Fuckers," Quinn snarled, but dropped his hands to his sides. "Don't hurt her. Don't hurt any of them. Look, you want cash? I can get you some."

"Shut up," he answered. "Get the girl," he instructed the man pointing his gun at Luna. "She's the only one we need. We can't fuck this up or the client won't pay us the rest of the money."

The man yanked Luna to her feet and although she wanted to recoil from his touch, she followed him meekly.

"What do we do with everyone else, Boss?" Quinn's attacker asked.

The ringleader looked around. "There—put them in the closet!"

He pushed his gun at Quinn and grabbed Selena by the arm, pulling her to her feet. He opened the closet and shoved them both in followed by Evie. Closing the door, he jammed a chair against the knob to secure it.

"Let's get outta here."

They left the office, Luna in tow, and headed towards the elevator. The ringleader pushed the call button impatiently. "Fucking old thing."

The elevator heaved and clanged, signaling the approaching car.

"Finally." The ringleader grabbed the cage door and pulled it open. "Get in," he said to Luna, pointing the gun at her.

Before she could comply, something very large and fast leaped out, pushing her forward into the elevator. The metal cage door screeched as it shut in front of her face. She grabbed at the bars, desperate to see what was happening.

"Connor," she cried in surprise, recognizing him immediately. She had never seen a man so big move so quick.

He grabbed two of the men at the same time, lifted them up in each hand, and knocked their heads together sending them to the ground in a heap. He turned around, and Luna felt a chill creep up her spine when she saw his face. It was a cold mask, eyes dead as he stalked toward the ringleader.

The man cried out as Connor grabbed his collar and lifted him up all too easily before smashing his face with a giant fist. The sound of bones breaking and blood splattering made Luna's stomach turn and she sank to her knees, unaware that tears were streaking down her face.

She was too scared to look up, too afraid of what she'd see next. The grating of the metal door as it opened made her teeth hurt.

"Are you all right?" Connor's voice was eerily gentle. He was bent down to her level and Luna forced herself to look at him. His face seemed normal now, concern marring his features. She nodded shakily.

"What happened?" he asked as he helped her up. "Where's—" His expression changed and he whipped around. "Fuck!" he cursed and stalked down towards the office.

Luna followed him as quickly as she could though it was impossible to keep up with his long strides. When she entered the office, he was already opening the closet door.

There was a cry, a curse, a yell, and then three figures came spilling out. Evie was first, falling forward, but Connor caught her, his tree-trunk arms wrapping around the brunette to steady her.

"Stop trying to cop a feel, asshole!" Selena yelled at Quinn as she stumbled out of the closet.

"I wasn't trying to molest you," he protested, raising his hands. "There wasn't any room in there. I couldn't even breathe. Next time, lay off the perfume, huh?"

"Fuck off," she retorted. "Luna! I thought they'd taken you. Are you all right? The baby! Do you need to go to the doctor?"

Luna let Selena drag her to the couch. "I'm fine," she said, pushing the other woman's hands away. She seemed determined to examine her.

"Sorry," she said with a nervous laugh. "I'm kind of a worry wart. It's that nurturing nature witches have."

"Some witch you are," Quinn said. "Couldn't even get us out of the closet."

"I'm not that kind of witch," Selena shot back. "Besides, if you weren't thinking with your other head, we could have gotten out of there sooner."

"Hey, what do you mean—Yo, Connor!" Quinn turned to his

brother. "Thanks for the save. I think you can let go of Evie now."

The couple quickly disentangled themselves from each other.

"I have a boyfriend!" Evie blurted out, flapping her hands at Connor.

"Not anymore," Selena cackled. Evie shot her a glare, but the redhead shrugged. "You told me you guys broke up. Again."

"Shut up, Selena." Evie's entire face was a crimson color and she staggered back to her desk.

Connor, on the other hand, let out a grunt and turned to Quinn. "What the fuck happened here?"

Quinn relayed the story to Connor, the latter seeming to get more agitated as he listened. "Fucking hell. What do they want with you?" he asked Luna.

"I don't know," she whispered, her hands dropping to her stomach.

"First you were attacked coming home, and then they come barging after you," Connor gruffed. "What aren't you telling us?"

"You're scaring her," Selena countered. "Stop it."

"Chill, bro," Quinn said. "It's not her fault that someone's out to get her."

Luna's heart continued to thunder in her chest. It was suddenly sinking in how much danger she was in, and what would have happened if Connor hadn't been there. Who was trying to kidnap her?

"Fuck!" Connor rubbed his hand over his face. "I left those bastards out there!" He moved quickly, darting out the door. "Quinn!" he called out and the other Lycan ran outside.

"Are you sure you're okay?" Evie asked as she walked towards Luna. "I'm fine," she rubbed her hand over her stomach.

"They got away," Quinn said as he popped his head into the office. "Evie, call Sebastian. We need to get in touch with Killian ASAP." The brunette nodded and immediately reached for the phone.

"Everything will be all right," Selena told Luna, putting an arm around her. She didn't even realize she was shaking. Suddenly, all she wanted was to be in Killian's arms. To have him embrace her and tell her she was going to be okay. He'd only been gone for a day and she was already missing him.

Connor stalked inside, Quinn right behind him. "She all right?" he asked Selena.

"I think she's in shock," the redhead replied. "I have some tea in my bag. It's a special family blend. Let me make some for you." Selena stood up and walked to the pantry in the back of the office.

"Did you recognize any of those guys?" Quinn asked as he sat down next to her, his face serious.

She shook her head. "No. They're not the same guys from the other night."

"It sounded like they were paid goons," he observed.

"I don't understand," she whispered. "Why would anyone want to hurt me?"

"How many times now? Twice?"

She nodded. "No, wait." Ice filled her veins. "Two days before I came here was the first time. The reason why I followed Killian was that I'd been hit by a car, but nothing happened to me."

"Wait," Quinn shot to his feet. "You got hit by a car?"

"It was a hit and run. I was scared because I didn't have any money for an ambulance, so I ran."

"But you think it wasn't an accident."

"I...I don't know. It was too fast."

"I'll look into it. Where did it happen?"

"I was crossing Canal Street. Maybe it was at Forsyth? I was walking home." She gave Selena a nod of thanks as she accepted the hot cup of tea from the other woman.

"All right, doll," he soothed. "I'll find out more."

"Quinn," Evie called as she put the phone down.

"Did you talk to Killian?"

She shook her head. "He's still in the blackout site. But Mr. Creed said he'd get the word out as soon as possible."

"Good. Killian's gonna lose his shit, but it's better they tell him sooner than later."

11

Killian was bone tired by the time the Creed Security team extracted him from the black site. However, when he heard what happened at the office, he demanded to be sent back to New York City. He would have swum across the ocean if that was faster, but thankfully Sebastian had anticipated his reaction and had his private jet on standby.

Despite the luxurious cabin of the plane, Killian couldn't sleep a wink. His inner wolf was anxious and pacing back and forth. It needed Luna—to know she was okay. Hell, he just needed her. His blood ran cold each time he thought of what could have happened to them all in his absence. His mind also raced trying to figure out who would hurt Luna. He vowed that he would find out and stop those sonsabitches.

Sleep continued to escape him, though he did drift off for a few minutes here and there. As soon as the plane landed in New York, he raced back to the city.

"She's in the guest room," Meredith said as he entered the loft. His sister was in front of the TV, watching some reality show about housewives.

"Thanks," he called. "And put a damn security system in your apartment!"

"I am the security system," Meredith retorted.

He stalked down the hallway to Luna's bedroom, flinging the door open. She was curled up in bed, a book in her lap. She startled, but when she saw him in the doorway, she tossed the book aside and hopped off the bed, running to him.

"Killian," she whispered as he swept her up into his arms. Her skin was blotchy and eyes red from crying.

"Sweetheart," he said, the knot in his chest finally loosening. The wolf calmed down too as soon as Luna's cinnamon scent hit his nose. His hand went to her stomach possessively while his other hand dug into her hair and pulled her head back so he could kiss her. She tasted sweet and her lips made his head swim. The thought that he could have lost her made anger creep back into his veins.

"Goddammit," he cursed, and he tightened his grip. "I'm going to kill them. I'm going to find whoever's doing this to you and I'm going to kill them all."

"Killian, please," she said. "Don't do anything rash."

"Rash?" he roared. "I'm not going to stand here and do nothing. They can't hurt what's mine and get away with it."

"Getting yourself killed won't do any good. Just calm down and we'll go to the police."

"The cops? Are you kidding me?" he asked, raising his voice. "The NYPD won't be able to do anything about this. We have to take matters into our own hands."

"Are you a vigilante now?"

"This is about protecting you, sweetheart," he countered. "Now, grab your things. We're gonna head to my place. I'll have a security system in place by tonight."

"Killian—"

"And you're gonna stay there until we find out who's out to get you."

"Killian—"

"You're going to quit your job at the gallery."

"Killian, listen to me!" she yelled, pushing her palms hard against his chest.

"What?" he asked. "Are you going to say no? Someone's out to get you! God knows what they're planning."

"That doesn't mean you get to control my life." She stomped back to the bed and plopped herself down.

Killian curled his hands into fists. Why was she so stubborn? He calmed himself and thought back to Meredith's words. Maybe it was time he and Luna had an adult conversation. It was something he'd been dreading and trying to avoid. He didn't want to talk. Because he thought that maybe if he moved her into his place and distracted her with sex, she'd want to stay. Any scenario where Luna could not be his was just unthinkable at this point.

"Luna—"

"Ask me what I need, Killian."

"What?"

She turned her head to face him, her gaze dead serious. "I said, ask me what I need."

He sighed. "What do you need, Luna?" And don't tell me to leave you alone, he pleaded silently.

"I need normalcy," she said in a defeated tone. "I want to feel normal. No shifters, no kidnappers, no magical babies. I just need things to be normal. Even just for a second."

Normal. He felt the tension leave his body. He could work with normal. "All right. Be ready by seven."

"Huh?" Her brows furrowed as she looked up at him.

"I'm taking you out," he stated. "On a date. Like a normal couple." Before she could protest, he left the room.

Luna was worried because she didn't have any clothes or makeup for their date, but of course, she didn't have to worry. Meredith and Jade arrived soon after Killian left, carrying bags and clothes.

"I have lots of maternity clothes you can borrow," Jade said as she took out sweaters, leggings, dresses, and various articles of clothing from one of the paper bags. She set those aside then took out a white box. "You're about a month behind me which means you can have this." She opened it, taking out a black, lacy negligee.

"Jade, you slut!" Meredith said gleefully.

"It's brand new," Jade said, handing it to Luna. "La Perla's maternity line. Hasn't even been released yet."

The fabric was silky soft and the lace trimming around it was gorgeous. The front was split open so that it could be worn even late into pregnancy. There was also a matching pair of panties inside the box. "I can't possibly wear this. This must have cost a fortune."

"It's yours," the other woman said. "Sebastian would have just ripped it apart."

"Yeah and now Killian can tear it to shreds," Meredith added.

Luna blushed. Of course, she knew that there was a possibility that they would end up in bed. And frankly, she didn't have the emotional strength to fight whatever direction she and Killian were headed.

After trying on a couple of outfits, the girls finished dressing her up. They settled on a cute violet sweater that enhanced her eyes and black leggings with dark brown boots. She wore the lingerie of course, after much coaxing from the two Lycan women. Meredith helped with her makeup, applying just enough to enhance her features.

Killian showed up at seven on the dot looking handsome in a pair of dark jeans, a sweater, and a thick leather jacket. He also brought a bouquet of orchids, her favorites (she didn't even want to think how much it cost to get them in winter), which Meredith had put in a vase for her.

"Don't do anything I wouldn't," Meredith yelled at them as they were leaving. "And that's not a lot."

Killian rolled his eyes as he closed the door behind him.

"Where are we going?" she asked as he helped her into his Jeep.

"Dinner," he said. "And maybe a late movie, if you're not tired? There's a French film festival on the Upper East Side."

"Sounds lovely," she replied.

He took her to a cozy little Spanish restaurant. It was upscale, but not too fancy, and they ate small plates of food, though Killian ordered two of everything on the menu. Luna surprised herself at how much she could eat. A rush of pink stained her cheeks when she saw the number of empty plates their poor waiter had to clear, but Killian gave her a reassuring smile and pat on the hand.

All in all, the date was normal. Discovering the existence of Lycans gave Luna some relief—at least the part where her baby was safe and there was nothing wrong with her—but it had sent her life into a tizzy. Werewolf shifters, warlocks, witches—it was all too much, not to mention the cherry on top of someone trying to kidnap her. She longed for the boring, routine life she had, which is why she just wanted to do something normal.

Killian finished paying for their meal then turned to her. "Ready for that movie?" he asked with a smile.

Her heart somersaulted in her chest. "No."

He frowned. "No?"

"No, I don't want to see a movie," she said in a quiet voice. She mustered up all her courage. "I want to go to your place."

Killian's frown turned to surprise then a flash of lust crossed his face, sending her hormones into overdrive. He practically dragged her out, not bothering to wait for his change, and soon they were in his Jeep. They pulled into his building and she suppressed a laugh realizing he didn't live that far away from her.

As he pulled into his parking spot, Luna had a sudden feeling of fear. It had been months since she'd been with him and he'd yet to see her naked. Would he want to make love to her now?

"What's wrong?" he asked as he helped her out.

"I'm…" What could she say? She suddenly felt shy. "I'm huge," she said, trying to turn away from him. "And I'm only going to get bigger."

"You're beautiful," he countered, turning her head back to him and running his fingers down her cheek. "Always have been. Always will be." He leaned down again to kiss her, pressing his lips to hers. "I want you." To make his point, he grabbed her hand and brought it between his legs, making her palm press over the large bulge there. "I've had this hard-on since I picked you up. Hell, I've had it since I saw you again."

She sighed against his mouth. God, she wanted him too. "We probably need to be careful with the baby, right?"

"I know there might be some positions that we can't do," he said. "But I've done some research. We can try a few things."

Killian doing pregnancy sex research? That made her smile. "All right then, show me."

He tugged her towards the elevators which were thankfully empty, wrapped an arm around her waist and pulled her to his side, but didn't do anything more. She guessed there were cameras overhead.

He led her to his apartment, opened the door and let her go in first. The main living room was spacious, if a little bare, and the large windows had a magnificent view of Manhattan.

"I—Killian!" She giggled when he swept her off her feet. "I'm heavy."

"You weigh nothing at all," he said, walking her into his bedroom. He lay her down on the bed gently then unzipped her boots and tossed them away. He crawled over her, lying down next to her as she smoothed her hair away from her face.

"I'm sorry," he said, lowering his eyes. "I'm sorry I wasn't there to protect you."

"You're here now," she said. "That's all that matters."

He leaned down and his mouth covered hers hungrily. The kiss sent spirals of hunger and lust through Luna's body, making her dizzy.

"Killian," she moaned as she felt a hand slip under her leggings.

"Luna, I need you," he said. His fingers traced over the silky panties and his pupils blew open. "What are you wearing under here?" he rasped, his voice thick with desire.

"Why don't you find out?"

Killian made quick work of her leggings, pulling them down and off her legs. He straddled her between his legs then grabbed the bottom of her sweater and brought it up over her head. His gaze raked over her, devouring the sight of her body in the lacy black lingerie.

"Do you like it?" she asked shyly.

"I love it," he growled. He slipped his jacket off, then his sweater, leaving his muscled chest naked. Her eyes followed his hands as he unzipped his jeans, shucking them off quickly. His cock was already hard, the tip bobbing against his flat stomach and she suppressed a moan, but the flaring of his nostrils indicated he could smell her arousal. His hands cupped her breasts through the lace, caressing them gently. Pulling the cups of the bra top down, he leaned down and popped a nipple into his mouth.

"*Killian,*" She dug her fingers into his hair, raking her nails gently into his scalp. She remembered how much he loved that and he responded by sucking on her nipple harder. "Oh, yes...don't stop!"

His hand moved lower, exploring her thighs and teasing her skin, sending desire straight to her core. When his fingers pulled her panties aside and traced her wet slit, she moaned and bucked against him. He slipped a finger inside her with ease and her pussy tightened around him.

"Oh, yes," she moaned, moving her hips along with the slow thrusts of his fingers.

"You're fucking soaked, sweetheart," he murmured against her breast. "Do you need to cum?"

"Yes," she nodded. "Please make me cum, Killian."

He slipped another finger inside her and twisted his palm so the heel ground against her clit. Her hips lifted up from the bed, the pleasure zinging throughout her body. She opened her mouth to scream, but Killian covered it with his, his tongue exploring her mouth. Her body tensed, sending her over the edge. His mouth continued to devour hers, sucking on her tongue as her body relaxed.

"Beautiful," he said.

"I want you now. Please, Killian."

"You don't have to beg, sweetheart," he replied, pushing her gently to her side and slipping the panties off her. "You never have to beg me." He slid his body against her, his warm skin pressing against her back and slipped an arm under her. She parted her thighs as the tip of his cock nudged at her entrance from behind. "Just tell me if you're uncomfortable or in pain and we'll stop, okay?"

She nodded.

Slowly, he pushed inside her, and Luna held her breath. God, it felt so good, after all these months. She grabbed onto his forearm and pushed herself back to take him all in.

"Fuck, Luna," he rasped against the soft skin of her neck. "You feel so good. Everything okay, baby?"

"Yes," she groaned. "Please don't stop."

He moved slowly, tentatively at first. Luna whimpered with need when his hand moved between her thighs and found her clit. He pinched gently, sending a convulsion through her body as she bucked back against him, meeting his every thrust. It was incredible, just like she'd remembered and even better. She rocked back against his cock and this time, he was the one who let out a groan.

"So good, baby," he whispered in her ear. "Your pussy is so hot and tight. Fuck, I want to cum in you." His fingers ground against her clit and he sank deeper into her. It was what sent her careening over the edge, and she pulsed around him. The orgasm hit her so hard and fast her ears buzzed. He let out a grunt and she felt his cock pulse, emptying his seed inside her. Killian clutched her tightly as he bucked into her, coaxing one more shiver of pleasure from her before he relaxed.

He kissed her neck, licking at the skin, as if he didn't mind the soft sheen of sweat covering her. When his cock softened and slipped out of her, she felt the cold air on her back as he left.

"Killian?" she turned around and saw the light in the bathroom. He came out moments later, a cloth in his hands.

"Let me clean you up, sweetheart."

She sighed when he parted her thighs and the wet, warm cloth made contact with her skin. It was soothing and when he finished, he lay down, curling himself around her. With one arm wrapped around her middle and a large hand over her belly, his breathing evened out and he fell fast asleep.

As she lay in his arms, her mind was racing. Killian wanted her and their child for sure. But what about afterward? When the novelty of being together wore off and their child was born? Things would change and real life would take over. Then there was the fact she hadn't heard him mention the one thing her heart was aching to hear. And she wanted to hear those words because she was pretty sure that she was in love with him. She always had been, since that first date.

She pressed her face into the crook of his neck and breathed in his scent. Even if she couldn't have Killian's heart, then maybe she would at least have this.

12

The next day, Killian woke up early and made her breakfast in bed. It took two trays to bring everything in, but Luna found herself finishing up the pancakes, sausages, and eggs that he made. When he put the used dishes aside, he gave her a naughty grin and proceeded to show her more of the sex positions he had read about. Needless to say, as she lay boneless and utterly satisfied, she was impressed with his research skills.

"I have to go into the office," he said, giving her a kiss as he got up from the bed. "I have things to take care of and a meeting with the boss. I'll be back as soon as possible. But, I need to ask you a favor."

"A favor?"

"Well, I've been living here for a while, but as you can see, it's not much of an apartment," Luna recalled that the living room had been bare with only a couch and large flat-screen TV. "Sebastian's always sending us on ops abroad so I haven't had time to furnish the place. Could you do some shopping today and get me some furniture?"

"Uh…I guess?" Not like she was busy. She had already

decided to give her notice at the gallery too. If danger was following her then she couldn't risk any more innocents hurt. She might be invincible, but everyone around her wasn't.

"Good. Evie and Meredith will come by to help you," he said. "I'm gonna hop in the shower and get ready." Killian disappeared into the bathroom and Luna lounged back in the bed, enjoying the smell of Killian and their lovemaking on the sheets.

A few minutes later, he stepped out, a towel wrapped around his waist. Luna's mouth went dry at the sight of his bare chest and the droplets of water clinging to his skin.

"Stop looking at me like that," he growled.

"Like what?"

"Like you want to eat me," he said. "Unless you want me to drag you into the shower?"

She chuckled. "Maybe tonight." With a saucy grin, she got up from the bed and grabbed his shirt from the floor. Now that she was somewhat decent, she decided to go out into the living room to see what she had to work with.

While the view was impressive, the living room itself was bare. Aside from the couch and TV, the only other piece of 'furniture' (and she was loath to call it that) was a milk crate that was standing in for a coffee table.

She suppressed a grin, thinking of Killian living a bachelor lifestyle, sitting on his couch and watching sports, maybe eating takeout. A surge of jealousy suddenly went through her though at the thought of just how much of a bachelor lifestyle he'd been leading all these months. It made her stomach twist, but she tamped it down. They'd been apart all this time, and she couldn't blame him if he needed female company. Still...

"What's wrong?" he asked as he stood in the doorway to the bedroom.

"Nothing," she replied.

Killian stalked over to her, barefoot but dressed in his usual jeans and sweater. "You smell mad."

"Can you really smell that?"

"Something like it," he said. "Your body is tense and I can tell something's bothering you. Now please—talk to me."

"It's silly," she said with a forced laugh.

"It's not if it's bothering you," he said, crossing his arms over his chest.

"I was just thinking…how many other women you've had over here."

He let out a sigh and then gathered her into his arms, resting his chin on the top of her head. "Zero," he assured her. "I haven't been with anyone since you. Unless you count my girlfriend since I was a teenager, Pamela Hand-erson." He raised his right hand.

She laughed. "Really?"

"Really," he kissed her forehead.

"I haven't been with anyone else," she confessed. "Just so you know."

"Good," he said. "Now, should I show you—"

A knock on the door made her head turn.

"Ah, they're here," Killian said, as he let go of her and walked over to the front door to open it. "Thanks for coming."

"Sure thing, Boss," Evie said as she walked in, followed by Meredith. "Wow, you do need help," she observed, her eyes looking over the apartment. "Hi, Luna," she said with a wave.

"How was your date?" Meredith added, flashing Luna a wink.

She blushed. "It went well."

"I bet."

"Evie's dad owns a furniture store," Killian explained. "I figured she'd be able to help you pick out some good stuff."

"And I'm here to help you spend my brother's money," Meredith cackled. "We'll make a dent in his bank account."

Killian chuckled. "You can try. Just make sure you get good furniture. I want sturdy pieces that will last a long time." He walked back to Luna and gave her a kiss. "I'll be back tonight. See you then."

After he'd left, Meredith handed Luna more clothes from Jade. Some of them still had tags on, but the Lycan assured her that Jade had simply grown too large before she could wear them. She accepted them gratefully and went to the bedroom to change.

Evie came prepared with a list of furniture shops, and soon they were making their way to the first one on her list.

"Oh, this is nice," Luna said as she sank into soft, buttery leather of one of the sectional sofas. They were at a high-end home theater store on the Upper East Side which Evie recommended as the best one in the city. She looked around trying to find a price tag and when she couldn't find one, knew the store stocked only serious furniture.

"Do you like it?" Evie asked.

"Yes, but it must cost way too much."

"Killian wanted the best," Meredith said, plopping down next to her. "Ohhhh…" she moaned, rubbing her hands over the leather. "Oh yeah, we'll take this one."

Evie called the sales assistant over to help them and after a few words, the assistant took her to the back office to arrange the sale and delivery.

"I don't know why I'm the one making the decisions," Luna

said. "Killian should be doing this. Why is he sending us out to do his shopping for him?"

Meredith gave her a knowing grin. "Seriously?"

She frowned. "What? I know he's busy. I mean, the decor in his place is pretty sad and I get that he hasn't had time to do it himself. But surely he could pick stuff out from a website or something."

"Right."

The next store they went to were suppliers of upscale home décor. Luna had a lot of fun checking out the possibilities, reminding her of the time she was shopping for her apartment back in Portland. While a pang of sadness hit her at the loss of her old life, she somehow couldn't muster up the anger and hate she used to feel towards Killian. Is this what being in love was like? She wouldn't know, having never felt it before. In fact, she'd never had such intense feelings for anyone as she did for Killian.

"Earth to Luna," Meredith said, waving her hand.

"Oh sorry," she answered in a flustered voice. "I was thinking of something else."

"Thinking of last night?" Meredith said, wiggling her eyebrows. "Oh please. Spare me the details. I mean it—really. Don't tell me anything because he's my brother and that's just gross."

Luna chuckled. "I won't."

"Meredith, Luna," Evie called. She had walked ahead to another section of the room but backtracked. "Come here."

The two women followed, moving into the other room. Luna gasped, her eyes scanning the room. It was the nursery section and it was filled with cribs, bassinets, changing tables, rocking chairs, and other baby furniture. Seeing it all made something in her break and she began to sob.

"It's okay, it's okay," Meredith soothed, putting an arm around her.

"Oh my God, Luna, I'm sorry," Evie cried. "Did I do something wrong? I just assumed—"

"Pregnancy hormones," Meredith assured the younger woman. "Could you give us a minute? Why don't we meet you in the dining room section?"

The brunette nodded and hurried away, leaving the two women alone.

"What's wrong, honey?" Meredith asked.

"I...I..." Luna wiped her eyes with the back of her hand. What could she say? Her entire situation had suddenly hit her like an oncoming freight train. Her life was in shambles—no job, no home, baby on the way, and Killian? Well, that was a whole other mess. She shouldn't have gone out with him last night, nor slept with him. That small bit of normalcy had been what she needed, but now she was more confused than ever. Aside from the baby and sex, what did Killian want with her? What did she want from him?

Luna took a deep breath. "Like you said. Hormones."

Meredith looked at the nursery display. "It's all a bit much if you ask me. C'mon, let's get out of here."

Sebastian Creed frowned as Killian relayed what had happened when those men came for Luna. The former Marine-turned-CEO was obviously not happy that someone was able to breach one of his offices.

"You need to find out what happened, Killian," Sebastian said.

"We will," he vowed. "We can't let any of our competitors know we were easily attacked like that."

"Yes, that too. But I mean you have to find out whoever's trying to kidnap your mate," Sebastian added. "If your woman and pup are in danger, you have to put a stop to it. Use whatever means necessary. You have the office's resources at your disposal," he said as he stood up. "I have to go back. I'll make sure not to schedule you to go on longer trips until you have this thing sorted out."

"Thanks, Sebastian," he said as he stood up. "I'll see you around."

"Yeah, and Jade wants me to tell you that you guys are coming over for dinner some night. She and Meredith won't stop talking about your Luna." He grinned. "And I wanna see this girl who's gotten you wound up tighter than a monkey's nuts."

Killian chuckled. "Will do." He walked Sebastian out, promising to set a date when they could all have dinner. Closing the door behind him, he leaned back and closed his eyes.

"Killian, I need to show you something."

Killian's eyes flew open. Quinn's voice was serious, a rare occurrence. The expression on his face was grave, which made him even more edgy. Beside him, Connor looked grimmer than his usual self. "What is it?"

"Let's go to your office."

He followed his brothers down the hallway, and shut the door behind him. Quinn set up his pad on the table. "I found some footage. Of the hit and run on Luna."

Killian gritted his teeth. "Play it."

Quinn tapped the screen and a grainy video popped up. There weren't any details, but he could see the figure in the dark coat crossing the street, and all of a sudden, a dark sedan came from nowhere and hit the figure, sending it flying to the sidewalk.

"Turn it off!" His inner wolf was snarling and raking its

claws at his insides. He could feel it want to escape again and tear everything in sight.

"What the fuck were you thinking?" Connor growled.

"It's evidence," Quinn said. "It was obvious it wasn't an accident. That car meant to run into Luna. I have more footage of it waiting about a block down."

Killian let out a roar and slammed his palms on his desk so hard it left a dent. He took deep breaths, trying to keep the wolf at bay. *We'll get him,* he promised the wolf. *And when we do, you can do what you want.*

Heartbeats passed and finally, Killian felt calm enough to speak. "We need to find out who's behind this." He looked at Quinn. "I need to you to do a complete background check on Luna. We need to find out who's trying to kidnap her."

"Consider it done," he said.

"Good."

"What do you want me to do?" Connor asked.

"Nothing yet," Killian said. "But when the time comes..."

"I'll be there," the other Lycan replied as he stood up.

"Where are you going?" Killian asked.

"Out." The door slammed with a loud bang as Connor left.

"What the fuck is wrong with him?"

Quinn shrugged. "What the fuck isn't wrong with him?"

He shook his head and stood up. "I'm going home. Lock up when you're done, will ya?"

"Sure thing. Say hi to Luna for me."

Killian grabbed his jacket and headed to the parking garage. He hated driving in Manhattan, but he supposed he should get used to it. It was the middle of winter and Killian didn't want Luna to be taking the subway or cabs anywhere so from now on, he'd be driving her wherever she wanted to go. Plus, he got too antsy having to wait for public transport to get home. He wanted to be with Luna as soon as possible.

The traffic going uptown wasn't too bad and soon he arrived at his building. As he walked out of the elevator, his keen senses picked up some noise from his apartment, something he wasn't used to. It immediately made his wolf go on alert, but when he heard feminine voices, he let his guard down. Another thing to get used to, he supposed, but coming home to a noisy apartment was something he was looking forward to. It was sneaky of him to keep Luna in his home and make her buy his furniture, but what was he supposed to do? The damned woman was stubborn and proud, so he had no other choice but to move her in by stealth.

Killian unlocked the door and walked inside, listening to the woman chatting.

"Just you wait until it's your turn, Evie," Meredith giggled.

"Uh, no thanks," his admin said. "I mean, not yet. Maybe someday. But I'm trying to focus on my career for now."

Luna, Meredith, and Evie were sitting around a new coffee table which was piled with takeout boxes from the Indian restaurant around the corner. The two pregnant women had demolished most of the food while Evie picked at the plate of salad in front of her. Meredith pushed a container of naan at her.

"No thanks, I have to watch my figure," she added, wrinkling her nose.

"A certain someone didn't have a problem with your figure the other day," Luna giggled and Evie's cheeks pinked.

"What? Who?" Meredith's eyes darted from Luna to Evie. "What did I miss?"

"Don't you say it!" Evie warned.

"Well, I'm glad you're enjoying yourselves," Killian remarked as he entered the room.

"Killian," Luna greeted as she struggled to get up. He immediately went to her, placed his arms under hers and pulled her to her feet.

"Luna," he breathed, taking in her scent and pulling her close. It calmed him, calmed his wolf and holding her made the image of her body bouncing on the pavement disappear from his mind. Luna was here, she was alive.

"Do you like your furniture? Evie made sure they all arrived today."

"It's great. Thank you for getting that done." He bit his lip to stop himself from saying it wasn't just his furniture, but he buried his face in her hair instead. As he scanned the room, he saw that they had indeed gone to town, though he couldn't help but observe how everything was so masculine, from the brown leather couch to the wood console table in the corner, down to the maroon striped carpet. It was nice to have furniture again, but it looked too much like a bachelor pad. He would have liked a splash of color, maybe some of those doilies or blankets or whatever the hell women used to make things homier. He supposed though, as soon as Luna realized she was here to stay, she could redecorate to her heart's content.

"Great job, Evie," he said to his admin. He made a mental note to add a nice bonus to her next paycheck. Seeing Luna happy and laughing was worth it.

"Thanks, Boss!" She got to her feet. "I'll head out now. Thanks for the meal, guys," she waved as she headed for the front door.

"We definitely made a dent in your bank account," Meredith said as she reached for another samosa. "Luna has great taste."

Killian let go of Luna and grabbed the savory pastry from his sister, raising it high above his head.

"Hey, I was eating that!" She stood up and tried to grab it from him.

"Mer, you're my sister, and I love you," Killian said, "but you need to leave Luna and me alone now."

"Fine," she said when she snatched the samosa. She popped it into her mouth, chewed and swallowed it. "But I'm taking the naan with me." Meredith grabbed the last unopened takeout box. "I'll see you tomorrow, Luna."

"That was rude," she said as Meredith left.

"I needed to have you all to myself," he said, the urgency in his voice surprising him. He hated leaving her, especially after last night. He'd asked Meredith to stick to her from now on and while he was glad for his sister's help, he knew she would never leave if he didn't kick her out.

Luna let out a small yelp when he lifted her up into his arms. He sat down on the new sofa, sinking into the soft leather and positioning her so she straddled his lap. "Hmmmm...nice..."

"I thought you'd like the couch." She pushed aside a lock of dark hair that had fallen over his forehead.

"Yeah, that's nice too," he said as he brought her head down, crushing her lips to his. She sighed against him, pressing her body to his. God, she was magnificent, and he had missed just being next to her all these months. Her body had changed, yes, but she was silly if she thought he was turned off. He'd never wanted her more and it seemed so natural to see her body change as she grew their baby inside of her. A wave of possessive urgency swept through him, thinking of her confession this morning. Not that he could blame her if she sought out other lovers, but knowing she was completely and only his pleased that primal part of him.

"Killian," she gasped when he grabbed the bottom of her sweater dress and pulled it over her head. She wasn't wearing the lingerie from last night, but the pretty pink bra she had on now looked just as good. He unclasped the front hook, freeing her full breasts and sealed his mouth around a taut nipple. As his tongue lashed against the bud, she began to grind against him, sending all the blood from his brain to his cock. He could smell her arousal, the scent mixing with her delicious cinnamon pastry smell and he had to get inside her now.

"Luna," he said, putting his hands on her hips. "Slow down just a bit, sweetheart."

Her pouty pink lips parted and he thought of those times she had been on her knees, taking his cock in her wet mouth. One time, she blew him right in her office during lunchtime with all her coworkers just on the other side of her door. Killian groaned, his erection pressing against his jeans so hard it was painful. He quickly unbuckled his belt and popped the buttons on his jeans. His cock sprang free and Luna's soft palm wrapped around his length.

"Sweetheart," he moaned as she began to stroke him. His head rolled back and he closed his eyes. He let her jerk him off for a while, but when he was getting close, he had to stop her. "I need to be inside you."

"Yes," she moaned, and quickly discarded her leggings. When she tried to pull her panties down, he grabbed the scrap of lace and ripped them off then impaled her on his cock. She let out a soft cry as he began to fill her. He gritted his teeth as her slick passage wrapped around him, enveloping him. Gripping her waist, he pulled her down more and thrust up, making her yelp and dig her fingers into his scalp.

"Fuck, you feel so good on me," he gasped.

Luna threw her head back unable to speak as he continued to fuck into her tight little pussy and bringing her down on his cock at the same time. Her arms wound around his head, as if holding on for dear life. Her hot and wet cunt sucked at him, but he was desperate to hang on until she had her pleasure.

"Cum...for...me...sweetheart..."

"Killian, *oh*," Her body began to convulse, and her pussy fluttered around him, squeezing him tight. Hold on, he told himself. Just a few seconds more.

"Luna!" he called out as he pushed up as deep as he could go, emptying himself into her. He buried his face into her neck, nipping at her skin. That sent her shivering around him again, and her body shook with another orgasm.

She relaxed against him, her ragged breathing slowly becoming even as the seconds ticked by. "That was..." she whispered against his shoulder.

He smiled into her hair and then brought his hand between them, where their bodies were still joined. His fingers rubbed at her slick lips, still covered in her juices and his cum. "I know baby. And we're not done yet."

13

Killian was once again reluctant to leave her the next day, but he had to. Meredith arrived early, bringing more "borrowed clothes from Jade" that he had instructed her to buy. He hated lying to Luna, but his hands were tied. She was too proud to take his money, but it was obvious that she was in need of clothes. The maternity outfits she had in her closet at her apartment were all too small and threadbare. Besides, he loved seeing her in those sexy sweater dresses that showed off her curves and baby bump.

He kissed her goodbye and gave Meredith a playful scratch on the head like he used to do when she was little. As he drove to work, he vowed he would find whoever was trying to harm Luna and his child soon.

"Are you sure you're ready for this?" Quinn asked as they all sat around the small meeting room at the Lone Wolf offices.

Killian paused. When he and Luna had first met, he had toyed with the idea of doing a background check on her, but resisted. He wasn't out to use her to steal the tapestry at that time after all, plus he didn't want to invade her privacy. But, he supposed this was for a good cause. "Yes. Go ahead."

"Luna Rhoades," Quinn began as he pulled up the information on his tablet PC. "Twenty-five years old. Former place of employment, Portland Museum of Art. She was terminated four months ago following the theft of the famed *Gastlava Tapestry*." His brother raised an eyebrow at him.

Killian gritted his teeth. "We already know that. Keep going."

"Although the Portland PD didn't charge her with any crime, the owner of the tapestry, Larry Bakersfield, sued her in civil court for damages amounting to twenty million dollars." Quinn whistled. "She retained the services of Brian McGill, one of the top lawyers in the city and he was able to defend her resulting in the judge throwing out the case. Wow, I bet that must have cost her a pretty penny."

Killian felt lower than shit, and from the look Connor was giving him, his brother agreed. Guilt gripped him. The magnitude of what Luna had lost when he split was just hitting him now. Why Luna was still sticking around now was a mystery to him.

"What else?" he said, his hand gripping his coffee cup so tight, he feared it would break.

Quinn cleared his throat. "Well, I dug back further and…" He gave the tablet a tap and pulled up a mug shot of a man. "John W. Rhoades—Luna's father. He's currently serving a life sentence in the Arizona State Correctional Facility. Rhoades was a petty thief, previously did a nickel for armed robbery. When he got out, he did a big bank job with his usual accomplices, but he shot a cop hence the life sentence. Luna was two years old."

"Christ." Killian rubbed his palm down his face. Everything clicked into place now. His inner wolf was pacing again, urging him to go home and make sure Luna was still there, as if it was afraid she'd bolt anytime. All this time…he didn't know about her father.

"Hey, Kill," Connor said. "Focus. Think about that later. Remember what Archie taught us."

Killian nodded. "Compartmentalize." He took a deep breath. "So, what's your analysis?"

"Two possibilities," Quinn began. "First, maybe someone's out to get revenge on dad. Either an old accomplice or maybe someone on the inside."

"Or it could be Bakersfield," Connor added.

"Hmm...Bakersfield lost in court, but I'm sure he made off with the insurance payment," Killian said. "Besides, Luna doesn't have anything else he could take."

"So you're thinking of the prison angle?"

"Work on it," Killian instructed Quinn. "And let me know what you find out."

Killian spent most of the day locked up in his office, trying to rack his brain and remember any details from his time spent with Luna and the last few days to see if he could think of anything significant that could help him. But, his thoughts kept straying to the past and what he had done to her. The lawsuit, having to sell her apartment, and of course, her father serving time in prison. What a shit-show she had to deal with. He vowed to make it up to her, but somehow, he just couldn't think of anything he could do to restore her to her old life. And part of him didn't want to. He wanted to be selfish and keep her with him forever.

"Killian!" Quinn burst into his office, Connor hot on his heels.

The hairs on his arms stood on end. He knew that look on Quinn's face. He'd found something. "What is it? Did you find any more info on John Rhoades?"

He shook his head. "No. I mean, yes, but only to eliminate that angle. All of his accomplices from the robbery are either dead or on their last legs. And nothing significant on any prison inmates either. John Rhoades turned to drugs and became violent, so they put him in solitary for most of the last decade."

"And—what did you find?"

"This," Quinn showed him the screen of his tablet. "Larry Bakersfield has been in New York for the last week. I have his private jet logs to prove it. He's also secured the services of at least a dozen PIs all over the city. I hacked into some of their servers to look at invoices. He's been having her followed ever since she moved here."

A chill blasted through Killian and he gripped the edges of his table so hard his knuckles turned white. "What else? Anything significant?"

"Yeah, we really need to get better security for the office. For a security firm, we're pretty lousy at keeping ourselves safe," Quinn quipped, rolling his eyes. "Anyway, I picked up those guys who came in here on a couple of surveillance cameras around the block and got some good pictures of their faces."

Three mug shots showed up on the screen. Connor let out a soft growl as his eyes landed on the one in the middle.

"Jack Borden, Gene McConroy, and Marty 'Shorty' Alberts. Shorty was the guy who was in charge of the attack on the office. All career criminals with various arrests ranging from robbery to assault."

"Can we connect them to Bakersfield?"

"We sure can," Quinn said in a smug voice. "While Bakersfield paid his PIs with checks, he must have used cash for these guys. He withdrew a large amount from his bank in Portland just before he left and as soon as he landed..." Quinn pulled up another piece of footage. "Bakersfield met with Shorty the day before the attack here." There were two men on the screen, standing on a street corner. The footage was grainy, but Killian recognized Bakersfield. He handed the other man a large manila envelope. "Got this from a camera across the street.

We got lucky because they were meeting right in front of the British Embassy and security there is tight ever since those terror attacks. Right after this, Shorty headed over to Brooklyn and paid for four rooms in a seedy no-tell motel, and then they headed here."

"Fucking hell!" Killian cursed, slamming his fists on his desk.

"What do you wanna do now, Killian?" Connor asked. "Should we go get these guys?" His brother looked like he was ready for a serious fight.

Killian wanted nothing more than to wrap his hands around Larry Bakersfield's fat neck and watch his face turned blue. But, unless he was prepared to make Bakersfield disappear from this world, there would be consequences to assaulting such a prominent figure. It also wouldn't help Luna or give her her old life back. No, Larry Bakersfield had to be dealt with publicly. "Call the Alpha's office," he instructed Quinn. "We'll need the clan's connections for this one."

14

Luna and Meredith were out having coffee when they got an urgent call from Quinn. While he didn't give any details, he told them that they had to come to the Midtown NYPD station, *now*. Luna was worried that something had happened to Killian, but Quinn assured her no one was hurt. They rushed uptown right away and soon, they arrived at the police station.

"Luna! Meredith! Over here!" a familiar voice called out.

Luna's head turned toward the voice. Evie was standing in the lobby. Quinn and Selena were right beside her.

"What's going on?" she asked Quinn.

"We got him, Luna," Quinn said in a triumphant voice. "The bastard who's out to get you."

She gripped his arm. "Who is it?"

"Mr. Quinn?" An older, balding African-American man in a dark suit approached them.

"Just Quinn."

"Yes, right. I'm Captain Jackson. Are these the witnesses?" His sharp brown eyes scrutinized the women.

"Yeah, these three," he motioned to Luna, Evie, and Selena,

"were in the office at the time of the attack. The men indicated that Ms. Rhoades was the target."

Captain Jackson nodded. "All right, let's go. We need to take their statements and then they need to identify the suspects."

They followed the captain to the back room where the women gave their statements separately. Luna told the lead detective everything that had happened to her; from the hit and run to the attack on the office. Afterward, she went into another room where she had to pick out the three suspects in a lineup from behind a one-way mirror. She easily identified them, of course. There was no way she was going to forget those men.

It felt like days had passed, but it was only a few hours. A friendly female officer had helped her and given her some water and juice, but she declined any food. Though she was hungry, she couldn't bring herself to eat, not with her stomach in knots. She was sitting in one of the waiting rooms when Quinn came to get her.

"They don't usually let civilians watch interrogations," he said. "But we called Grant's office, and he called the Police Commissioner. He's aware of Lycans and so they're letting us keep close tabs on the investigation." Quinn led her to another room, and as soon as her eyes landed on Killian, she immediately went to him.

"It's almost over, Luna," he said as she embraced him tightly. Killian's body stiffened and then relaxed against her. She pressed her nose to his chest, letting his scent calm her down. She had been antsy and nervous the entire time she was in the police station, but she was determined to be brave. Now, all she wanted to do was crawl into bed with Killian and never leave.

"Who was it?" she asked. Killian nodded his head towards the one-way mirror, and Luna let out an audible gasp. "Bakersfield?"

Larry Bakersfield was sitting inside the interrogation room, wearing a smug expression. His lawyer was next to him, poker-faced, as the detective who she had talked to earlier calmly asked questions.

"But how?"

Killian gave her a brief rundown of what they had found out. After they had called Grant Anderson, he called the Police Commissioner who immediately assigned it to Captain Jackson's precinct. They picked up the suspects and as soon as the women identified them, all three began to talk. Not long after that, they picked up Bakersfield, right before he readied himself to leave New York.

"This is preposterous!" Bakersfield suddenly interjected.

"Larry, don't say anything—"

"I wasn't trying to kill her!" the hedge fund manager yelled. "I swear!"

"So, you admit to trying to kidnap her though?"

"I wasn't...I mean...I just..."

"You don't have to say anything Larry," his lawyer instructed.

"But I can't let them label me a murderer!" Bakersfield's face was red, his smug smile gone. "Detective, I just wanted to talk to the girl. She knows where my tapestry is—I know it! I knew it was just a matter of time before those two met up."

"So you know Mr. Jones?"

"Yeah, Jones or Smith or whatever his name is. You should be arresting him! Do you know the list of crimes he's committed? He's responsible for over a dozen major art and bank thefts all over the world, and *I'm* the one sitting here?"

"And you have proof of that?" the detective asked as he leaned back in his chair.

"Well, no. But I used all my underground connections to find out who could have stolen my tapestry and all my leads pointed to that man. He'd been dating Ms. Rhoades for some time and then disappeared as soon as the tapestry disappeared.

When she wouldn't give him up even after I sued her, I knew she was in on it. Probably had a big payday too."

Luna winced and Killian's body tensed up.

"So, what happened next?"

"I had PIs following her, waiting until she met up with him. And she did. When I got the report that she had made contact, I flew here."

"And you hired Mr. Alberts and his friends to kidnap her?"

"No!" he denied.

"We have proof Mr. Bakersfield," the detective said. "The British Embassy voluntarily gave us the footage from the security camera. You and Mr. Alberts met the morning of the attack on Lone Wolf Security."

"Purely circumstantial evidence," the lawyer answered. "My client could have been meeting him for any number of reasons."

"Ah, but we picked up the three suspects and they've confessed," the detective said.

"Fucking assholes!" Bakersfield exclaimed out loud. "I'm going to kill them!"

"Larry, don't say another word," the lawyer ordered in a sharp tone. He turned to the detective. "The girl wasn't harmed, nor was she kidnaped. Even if they identify my client, I could argue that it was attempted."

"Oh, but then there are the murder charges. Someone attempted to run over Ms. Rhoades a few nights ago. And we have it all on video."

"That wasn't me!" Bakersfield roared. "I swear! I didn't want her harmed or killed. I just wanted to know what they did with my tapestry."

The detective shook his head. "Our investigation will continue, but for now, we have enough to charge your client."

"We'll make bail."

"*If* the judge grants him bail. Did you know that Ms.

Rhoades was pregnant, Mr. Bakersfield? That's an attempt on two lives."

Bakersfield screamed in anger and his lawyer tried to keep him calm again. Luna couldn't stand it. She had to get out of there. She quickly ran towards the door, heaving and trying to get as much air as possible into her lungs.

Larry Bakersfield had been having her followed all this time. What did they see and know about her? She suddenly felt vulnerable and naked, and the bile was rising from her throat.

"Luna." A hand touched her shoulder, and she immediately knew who it was.

"It's over, right?" she asked. "He's going to go away?"

"I'll do whatever I can to make sure he gets jail time," Killian assured her.

"But...do you think he's telling the truth? Is there someone else trying to..."

"I don't know," he said. "But if there is, I'm going to get them, too."

15

The rest of the evening went by in a blur. They all stayed another couple of hours, just to make sure the police charged Bakersfield. Luna assured the detectives she would be willing to cooperate and testify every step of the way. After a quick dinner, she followed Killian into his Jeep, not even protesting or assuming she was going anywhere else.

Killian seemed withdrawn the whole time, but she shrugged it off. He was probably tired. She was too, emotionally drained from the whole saga, but when he flinched as she threaded her fingers through his under the table at dinner, she knew something else was up. Was he hiding something from her?

"I need to take care of a couple of things," he said as they entered his apartment. "Go on and get some rest."

A cold wave of emotions washed over her. This was the first time in two days Killian wasn't eager to have sex with her. She was exhausted, but all she wanted was to forget what happened and be in his arms. With a resigned sigh, Luna went to the bedroom, took a shower and dressed in one of Killian's white cotton t-shirts, wanting to have his scent around her if he wasn't next to her in bed. Meredith had explained today that as True Mates, Killian should smell particularly good to her and she to him. She had made a mental note to ask him what she smelled like to him, but she had forgotten with all the excitement.

She lay in bed, tossing and turning, unable to get any sleep. It was past midnight according to the clock on the bedside table, and still, he was nowhere in sight. What was the meaning of this? An inner voice whispered that maybe he didn't find her attractive anymore, sending a stab of hurt through her. Maybe that was it.

No freaking way. She refused to believe it. Not after all this time and not after she'd already fallen for him. She got up from bed and marched right into his office.

"Killian?" she spoke from the doorway . He was sitting behind his desk, his brows furrowed as he stared down at his laptop. The light from the screen etched the lines of worry deeper onto his face.

"Luna?" he looked up. "What are you doing up? You should be asleep."

"I couldn't sleep," she said. "Come to bed, please."

"I'm not done, yet. Go back to bed."

Luna bit her lip. "No." She walked over to him, determined to find out what was bothering him.

He pursed his lips and when she was standing right over him, he let out a sigh. "I'm doing some work. I need to do this. Please go back to bed."

"No. Not without you," she replied, her voice shaky.

Killian stood up and placed his hands on her shoulders. "This is important. I have to find out—"

"No—this is important." Luna reached up and wrapped her arms around his neck. She brought him down for a kiss and though he seemed startled at first, he responded, moving his mouth over hers.

When he pulled away, she clung to him. "Please, Killian, make love to me."

His gaze was hesitant for a moment, but then desire clouded over them. The look he sent her was almost feral. He grabbed her by the waist and planted her on the desk, pushing his laptop aside in one motion. He caught her mouth in a rough kiss, his lips almost bruising. Hands pushed the hem of her shirt up and her panties down to her ankles.

He groaned when he found her already wet and ready. She parted her thighs and he pushed her down on her back, raising her legs, so her feet lay flat on his desk. The sound of his belt unbuckling made her shiver.

"Killian," she cried out when he thrust into her in one motion. She closed her eyes, biting her lip as Killian began to move inside her, dragging the length of his cock along her tight passage. His fingers found her clit and one touch sent an orgasm ripping through her.

He didn't slow down, pummeling deep and fast into her. She hung on to the edge of the desk, meeting his every thrust. Her second orgasm was building and it wasn't long before she came again, sending ripples of pleasure all the way to her toes.

As she came down, she looked up at Killian. His face was taut, almost like he was in pain. Still, he continued to plunge into her, and while she felt the edges of a third orgasm approaching, she realized he was holding off on his own pleasure.

"Killian."

He wasn't paying her any attention. His fingers found her clit again, coaxing a small shudder from her body. She thought he would cum, but he wasn't stopping. The pain on his face was evident now. What was he doing? He was gritting his teeth and his eyes were closed, the tension on his face obvious.

"Killian, please," she moaned. "Fuck me," she urged. "I want your cum in me. Or do you want to come on my tits? Or in my mouth? I know you like that."

He let out a roar and thrust into her one last time, his cock twitching as he spilled inside her. She wrapped her legs around him and he pushed deep, grunting before bracing his palms on the desk to support himself. His ragged breaths slowed down, then he withdrew from her, stepping back as he helped her sit up.

"Killian. Look at me."

Turquoise eyes stared into her. She wasn't sure what he was feeling right now, but it wasn't satisfaction, and it wasn't happiness. He broke eye contact but gathered her into his arms.

"What's wrong? Talk to me, please?"

He didn't say a word but lifted her up instead, carried her out of his office and padded softly into the bedroom. Silently, he lay her down, slipped in beside her and pulled the covers over their bodies.

As Luna lay next to him, a dreaded feeling crept into her heart. Something was not right, she knew it. And she was determined to find out what.

Waking up alone in the morning did nothing to abate Luna's suspicion that something was going on with Killian. When she woke and realized he was gone, worry began to creep into her mind again.

Meredith and Evie came around so they could finish shopping for the apartment. But as they walked around the bedding section of Bendel's, it was evident Luna's heart was not into the excursion, so Meredith promised them both the best Italian food in all of Manhattan. She even told Evie to ask Selena to come along; a free meal was the least they could give her after all, considering all the trouble the redhead went through.

Selena was already waiting for them, and the four women walked into Muccino's Italian restaurant.

"I didn't know the Lupa owned a restaurant and that her brother was a chef," Evie said as they walked inside. "And they're right around the corner from the office."

"One of the reasons Killian chose the office location," Meredith said. "Hey, Enzo," she greeted the tall, handsome man standing next to the host's station inside the restaurant.

"Hey ba—I mean, Meredith," Enzo Muccino greeted back. "Um, is your husband around?" he asked, his eyes darting around.

Meredith giggled. "No, don't worry, he's not with us."

"Good," he said with a nod.

"Are you afraid of Daric?" Meredith asked with a grin.

"No," he denied. "I was afraid you guys were going to bang in the bathroom again," he said, rolling his eyes. "I need to warn my staff so you don't traumatize them. Again."

Meredith slapped him on the arm playfully. "Aww, c'mon. It's not like your busboy needed therapy."

"Say, did you guys pop in there for a quickie the other night? I could have sworn I heard something while we were closing up."

"What?" she asked innocently, batting her eyelashes. "I don't know what you're talking about." But as Meredith turned away from Enzo, a smile was tugging at her lips.

"Right. Well then," he nodded at the rest of the women. "Ladies, we've been expecting you. Frankie's not here right now, but she said you're our VIPs for the day and she picked out what you're going to eat, so come with me."

Enzo led them to a corner booth which already had bread,

olive oil and a few other appetizers on the table. "Your server will be with you shortly to take your drink orders. Have some wine too, if you like," He winked at Selena and Evie.

"Oh wow!" Selena grabbed the wine list. "Really? Maybe I should get kidnapped more often."

"You weren't kidnapped, Selena," Evie reminded her.

"Whatever. How about a glass of merlot?" she asked Enzo.

"Anything for you, sweet cheeks," Enzo replied. Evie shook her head when Enzo looked at her.

"No more wine for you, Evie-girl?" Selena asked in a teasing voice.

Evie shook her head. "Uh, never again. I've only gotten drunk one night in my life, and it was a big mistake."

"Next time Connor's being an asshole, please feel free to hit him with whatever object you have on hand," Meredith said. "Drunk or not." Meredith turned to Luna and explained what had happened the night Connor and Evie met for the first time.

"What were you doing at a male strip club anyway?" Meredith asked with a grin, elbowing Evie.

"It wasn't my idea!" She looked at Selena, who had put on her best innocent 'who me?' look.

"Excuse me, ladies," a deep voice said. Four pairs of eyes swung over the handsome man in the white chef's coat.

"Chef McHottie!" Meredith greeted, standing up and putting her arms around the man. "How have you been?"

"Oh you know," the chef said with a smile. "Same as always. Hello, I'm Dante Muccino," he nodded to the other women. Dante Muccino was gorgeous with his dark hair, olive skin and mismatched blue and green eyes. It wasn't surprising that Evie and Selena both were tongue-tied when the handsome young chef introduced himself.

"I'm E-evie," the brunette stuttered, extending her hand.

"I'm...I'm..." Selena's blue-gray eyes were boring holes right into Dante's face.

"Selena," Evie supplied, elbowing her friend.

The redhead's face brightened. "Yes. Selena. That's me. My name. Don't wear it out. Or wear it out, if you like. Haaaa..."

"And I'm Luna." She extended her hand and shook his.

"Well, Frankie told me to take care of you—"

"Oh will you, please?" Selena added, batting her eyelashes at him.

"Um, yeah," Dante chuckled. "Take care of your meal, I mean. So I whipped up some veal scallopini just for you. Off the menu. I'll have it right out, but in the meantime I'll send more appetizers and pasta to your table, okay?"

"Thanks, Chef," Meredith said with a jaunty, two-fingered salute.

"Selena, put your tongue back in your mouth," Evie ordered.

"Oh. My. God." Selena fanned herself. "He certainly deserves that nick name. Rreeowwl."

Luna laughed. She liked Selena, the almost-witch, and hoped she would be around more.

"So," Meredith began as she dished out some appetizers to the rest of the girls. "Luna, now that it's just us girls, tell us what's going on with you."

"What?"

"Oh come on," Meredith said. "When Evie and I arrived, you were moping around the house. And shopping didn't really seem to excite you, either."

Luna sighed. The three women looked at her with various expressions of concern and worry. She took a deep breath. "It's just...I feel like there's something wrong with Killian. With us. I think he's pulling away from me and I don't know why." Her throat tightened, and when Selena put an arm around her, she burst into tears.

"Aw, honey," Meredith said, offering her a napkin. "I'm sure he's just preoccupied. We're still not sure that your life is out of danger yet."

"He's pulling away from me." She wiped her eyes with the napkin. "I can feel it. Do you think he doesn't want me anymore? Am I getting too fat?"

"What?" Selena said. "You are not fat! Stop saying that."

"Maybe you're just reading things wrong," Evie offered. "I haven't known Killian for long, but he seems to be the serious type. Like, he just gets an idea in his head and he can't let go until it's resolved. So maybe Meredith is right and he's just got a lot of things on his mind."

"I am right. He wouldn't go to all this trouble to move you into his place, only to push you away."

Luna's mouth formed into a perfect 'o' at the Lycan's words.

"Oh, please," Meredith continued. "You haven't left his house since your date. He's bought you all these clothes so you have no excuse to go back to your place. For crying out loud, he's having you furnish his apartment. Nuh-uh, no," the blonde Lycan held her hand up when Luna tried to speak. "Yes, all that furniture is for you. I've already ordered the entire nursery set from that store, so don't you dare think he's going to toss you out. And if he does, he'll answer to me."

Luna sat silent, staring at her plate. Was Killian just distracted with work? Had he been moving her into his home all this time? Her hands went to her belly, and as if her baby heard her, she felt a small kick against her hand. She sighed. Maybe it was all her imagination.

Meredith continued. "Dante's coming back with our food. Just enjoy the meal, okay? Maybe when you go back home, you and Killian should have that serious conversation I've been telling you to have. Christ," she gave an exaggerated sigh. "I can't believe I'm the adult in this situation.

Luna nodded. Yes, it was time she and Killian had a sit down to talk about their future, and their child's. She only hoped he would say what she'd been hoping to hear.

16

Killian slammed his fist on the table in anger. Fucking hell. He ran his palms down his face in frustration. Hours and hours of research, reading and calling in favors, and still nothing. He let out a sigh and leaned back in his chair.

He had combed every piece of evidence they had and re-ran all the background checks on John Rhoades' accomplices and anyone he had been in contact with in prison, even the guards. Luna had mentioned that she and her mother had lived with a wealthy old couple, so he looked into their backgrounds too. He had a few possibilities, mostly disgruntled employees or business rivals, but nothing substantial.

While Larry Bakersfield was a bastard, Killian believed him when he said he didn't want Luna dead. Money motivated the hedge fund manager, and although he probably cashed in millions from the insurance money, Bakersfield wanted to have his cake and eat it too, so he had Luna followed. Besides, he wasn't from the streets, as evidenced by the way he conducted business with Shorty Alberts and his pals. Killian doubted the coward could stand the sight of blood.

And so here he was, back to square one. Someone was out to get Luna, but who? He would find out, and when he did, there was nowhere on earth the bastard would be able to hide. He would do anything to protect his mate and child.

But that wouldn't be enough. Killian had taken everything away from Luna, and he was doing everything in his power to make it up to her. He pulled his chair back to his desk and clicked a tab on the web browser. He was lucky that her apartment was still on the market. She had sold it back to the bank at a loss to pay for her legal fees, but no one had snatched it up yet. He spent all night talking to a real estate agent in Portland to make sure the sale went through. He didn't care how much it cost, just so long as it was done. As soon as he knew she was safe, he would give her the deed. With Larry Bakersfield's reputation being dragged through the mud with his arrest and possible trial, he knew it wouldn't be long before Luna's reputation would be repaired and she could have her old job back.

And when she decided to go back to Portland with their child? His inner wolf growled in protest. No, he told the wolf. He'd destroyed her life and she deserved a chance to have it back, even if it meant living with the hole in his heart for the rest of his life. Because that's what people do when they're in love, right? Set the ones they love free.

A ringing interrupted his thoughts and he fished his phone from his pocket. He frowned as he saw the caller ID read, 'unknown number.'

"Hello?"

"Lone Wolf," the raspy voice on the other end whispered.

A chill blasted through him. "Who is this?"

"It's not important who I am," the voice said. "But, it's important who I have."

"Is this a joke?"

"No, Killian. I finally have her. Your True Mate."

Luna. The wolf inside him howled in anger, its claws digging into him, begging to be let out. He felt the muscles twitch under his skin and he knew he was starting to lose control.

"Yeah, right." He had to reign the wolf in. "I'm hanging up now, asshole."

"Uh-uh, Killian," the voice warned. "Look outside."

Killian swiveled his chair around so he could see out the window. He looked down and saw a man in a dark jacket with a cap pulled low over his face. He waved at Killian and then jerked his thumb at the van behind him. The door slid open, and Killian saw a small figure with a flash of silvery hair tied up in the back. The door closed again.

"You fucking bastard! Who is this? I swear, I'm going to kill you—"

"Tsk, tsk, Killian," the voice taunted. "Come down now if you want to see her alive." The line went dead.

Killian ripped out of the office, slamming the doors open and not caring if they closed behind him. He didn't even wait for the elevators, running to the stairs and taking them two at a time. He let out a growl as the cold air hit him, and he felt the shift coming. Good. He and his wolf would rip those men who dared touch, Luna.

He stalked over to the van and pulled the door open. "Luna!" he cried as he saw her lying limply on the dirty floor of the van. He grabbed her legs to pull her out. "What the fuck?" He frowned, looking at the dismembered leg in his hand. He pulled the rest of the body out, only to reveal that it was a mannequin with a blonde wig. "Jesus—"

A puff of green smoke was the last thing he saw before the world went black.

17

"And so, Evie and her ex-boyfriend, Dick—"

"Richard," Evie corrected, "His name is Richard."

Selena took another sip of wine and ignored her. "So, anyway, *Dick*," she emphasized the name, "broke up over the phone with her all the way from Kansas, for like, the umpteenth time and I thought I'd cheer her up."

"By bringing her to a male strip club?" Luna asked.

"Hell yeah," Meredith raised her hand and Selena heartily high-fived her.

Luna shook her head. Their quick lunch had somehow turned into a three-hour affair, and Selena had already finished half a bottle of wine by herself. Totally sloshed, the redhead decided it would be fun to reveal all her best friend's secrets, much to Evie's mortification.

"Selena," Evie warned.

"C'mon, Evie, be a good sport," Selena said. "Look, we're trying to cheer up poor Luna. I'm sure she'll want to hear the rest of this story."

Luna chuckled. Growing up, she'd never had any close female friends. She never thought it was such a loss, but now she realized how nice it was to have people she could talk to and make her laugh. "Yes, please." She took a bite of the tiramisu. "Hmm, try this first, though. It's heavenly."

"Now, that is heavenly," Selena said as Dante Muccino came out of the kitchen to talk to some staff members. He was showing them something under one of the tables, and he bent over, showing off a well-formed backside.

Evie rolled her eyes. "Selena, you're impossible."

"What?"

"He's a Lycan. I thought you said you're—"

"*Pshaw,* a girl can dream, right?"

"Wait," Meredith interrupted. "Tell us the next part of the story of how Evie ended up at Merlin's and smacked Connor with her handbag."

"Oh, right," Selena giggled. "So, I told Evie to meet me at Merlin's that night and—"

"Selena!" Evie hissed and slapped her hand over the redhead's mouth.

Selena pulled the hand away. "Evie, what the he—llo, boys!" She greeted brightly.

Luna turned her head. Connor and Quinn were standing right behind them. Both wore serious expressions on their faces.

"Have you seen Killian?" Quinn asked.

"Not since this morning," Luna said. "I mean, early this morning. He left while I was asleep." A cold dread filled the growing pit in her stomach.

Meredith's back stiffened. "What's wrong?"

The two Lycans looked at each other then Quinn spoke. "We just came from the office. The doors were open and the lights were on, but Killian wasn't there. It was like he just left all of a sudden."

"Or was taken," Connor added.

"No," Luna cried. Selena put a comforting arm around Luna, but it did nothing to stop the icy fear filling her veins.

"Maybe he just went out?" Evie offered. "Were there signs of a break-in or struggle?"

"No," Connor said.

"Shit," Meredith stood up with such force that the table shook. "You know Killian wouldn't just leave like that."

"What's happening?" Luna asked. Her hand went to her belly. The baby was suddenly awake and she ran her palms over her stomach in a soothing manner.

Quinn let out a breath. "I think something may have happened to Killian."

They all headed back to Lone Wolf Security to try and piece together what happened to Killian. As soon as she saw his empty office with all the lights on, dread crept into Luna's heart. *No,* she told herself. *It couldn't be.*

"What was he working on?" Meredith asked as Quinn sat down in front of Killian's laptop.

"Hmmm...looks like he was doing more research on—" He stopped suddenly, but his eyes clashed with Luna's.

"What is it?" she asked, running to his side.

"He was looking into your father," Quinn said. "And into your mother's employers," he added quickly.

"He knew about my dad?" Luna asked, her voice quivering.

"I'm sorry Luna." Quinn lowered his head. "I had to do a background check to find out who was trying to kidnap you."

"But this doesn't make sense." Luna sank down on a chair, a look of disbelief on her face. "My dad's serving a life sentence. I doubt he even knows where I am."

"It was just an angle." Quinn stood up. "Wait here." He

leaped up from the chair and left the office, then came back seconds later with his laptop in tow. "We had security cameras installed just yesterday outside the building. I haven't had a chance to test them yet but..." He tapped the keys, and a window popped up on the screen, showing the outside of the building. "Let me scroll back...and there." Quinn swiveled his screen around. He tapped on the space bar, and the screen showed Killian running out of the building to a white van across the street. He opened the van's door and then suddenly collapsed. A man slipped out of the passenger seat and pushed Killian all the way into the back of the van, then shut the door. As soon as the man went back inside, the van sped off.

"Motherfucker!" Connor slammed his fist into the wall, his hand going right into the plaster. Quinn shut the laptop lid and began to pace. Meredith, meanwhile, was taking deep breaths. Evie and Selena looked at each other with worry.

"No!" Luna cried, clutching at her belly.

Selena put an arm around her. "Are you okay?"

"*Killian*..." The movement inside of her grew more restless as if the baby knew she was in distress. Someone had taken Killian, but who? How could they have fooled him?

"Has anyone found Killian's phone?" Quinn asked.

Meredith took her phone out of her purse and tapped on the screen. "I can't hear it anywhere. He's not answering either. But it's ringing."

"Good." Quinn set his laptop down and began rapidly typing. "Bingo!" He raised his fist in victory. "I'm glad Creed Security issued us those super phones. I can track him. It looks like they're still on the move. Heading East."

"Let's go," Connor said.

"I'm coming with you," Luna said, as she stood up.

"No way." Connor looked at her, his face dead serious. "You'll stay right here with Meredith and the girls."

"Hey, wait a minute!" Meredith put her hands on her hips. "What do you mean 'with Meredith'? I'm coming with you, dick-weed."

"You can't—"

"He's my brother!"

"And he's my mate," Luna said. "So I'm coming too."

"Are you insane? No fucking way."

"Luna and I are indestructible," Meredith reminded them.

"For fuck's sake." Connor's jaw clenched, and his eyes hardened. "You two are going to stay here, and that's final."

Quinn opened his laptop. "We should follow them now and see where they're taking him. Then, we can figure out what to do afterward. Evie," Quinn turned to the brunette, "call Creed and tell him what happened. We'll be right back after our scouting mission and regroup with him."

"Got it," Evie said, racing to her desk.

"Now, let's go track that van down. You all stay here and wait for word." Before any of them could protest, the two Lycans left.

"Are we really just going to stay here and do nothing?" Luna asked, wringing her hands. Killian was in trouble, and she just couldn't sit around.

"My brothers are stubborn, but I'm smarter and more evil," Meredith cackled. She tapped a message into her phone and a few seconds later, Daric materialized beside her.

"What's wrong, *min kjære*?" he asked, a worried mask marring his face. "Is it the baby? Are you all right?"

"I'm fine," she pouted. "It's my stubborn, asshole brothers."

"Holy shit balls!" Selena exclaimed, her jaw dropping. "You're a blessed warlock! What else can you do?"

Daric stared at the two women for a moment, and then a small smile began to tug at the corner of his lips. His ocean-colored eyes twinkled mischievously. "Hello, ladies. Nice to finally meet you. I'm Daric, Meredith's husband."

"And baby-daddy," she added. "Anyway, Daric, Killian's in trouble." She relayed what happened to her husband, who listened intently. "...And they just went off like that! The nerve."

"I'm sure Connor and Quinn are quite capable of doing a reconnaissance mission." Daric eyed his wife suspiciously. "All right, what do you want?"

"We," Meredith emphasized, looping her arm through Luna's, "want to come with them."

Daric crossed his arms over his chest. "And then what?"

"Well, we rescue Killian, that's what!" Meredith grabbed her husband's arm. "Please? Can you help us?"

The warlock let out a resigned sigh. "Fine. What is your plan?"

"Aww, thanks, baby!" Meredith gave Daric a kiss on the cheek. "Here's what we're going to do..."

18

Connor and Quinn were not happy when Daric, Meredith, and Luna appeared in front of the Range Rover.

"Motherfucker!" Connor cursed as the three of them casually hopped into the backseat. "Fucking hell, Meredith."

Meredith grinned. "I told you, we're coming with you. We probably won't even need anyone's help. Not with Daric on our side." She patted her husband's arm.

"Fine," Connor growled. "But you," he said to Luna, "will stay out of sight. Killian will have my hide if anything happens to you."

She nodded. "I just want to be there when you rescue him."

"Where are we, by the way?" Meredith asked, peering at Quinn's laptop.

"You don't know? How the hell did you get here?"

"Same way you did," she said. "Sebastian had you tracked and with satellite photos, Daric was able to transport us here. The dragon's on standby, but I told him we could all resolve this quietly. Now, what do we know?"

Connor gestured with a nod of his head. "We tracked Killian

to that mansion over there." The Range Rover was sitting across the street from one of the many mansions that dotted Long Island's coast. This one however looked like no one had lived in it for a long time. The shrubs around the property were overgrown and the rusty gate had a big padlock on it.

"We need to go get him," Meredith said. "Who knows what they could be doing to him now."

Quinn closed his laptop and looked back at Daric. "Can you get us in?"

"I'm afraid not," he replied. "I have never seen the inside of the mansion therefore I cannot transport us in there. I might be able to get us within the gates, but there is a risk of us materializing in front of a guard."

"Damn," Quinn cursed. "All right, we should maybe think of another way—" A loud tapping sound made Quinn's head snap back to his window. "Ah, fuck."

Outside, there were half a dozen men carrying guns surrounding the Range Rover. The man by the driver's side window tapped his weapon at the window again. Connor gritted his teeth and pressed a button on his armrest.

As soon as the glass went down, Quinn, Connor, and Meredith all tensed. Luna looked at Daric, but he remained silent, his eyes staring straight ahead.

"Lycan," Connor growled at the man.

"Get out of the car, all of you," he instructed, pulling the door open. "And don't even think of shifting. I'm sure our bullets will only slow you Lycans down, but what about your human companions?"

Defeated, they filed out one by one. The men around them kept their weapons trained at their group, ready to fire.

"Put the metal cuffs on them," the Lycan instructed. "And radio the boss. Tell them the prisoners are secure."

19

When Killian woke up, his head was throbbing like someone had put a jackhammer against his skull and went to town. He had only experienced this once before, so he knew there had to be magic at work. Were the evil mages back? No—they had destroyed them and their leader, Stefan. Of course, witches and warlocks also wielded magic, but that didn't make sense. As far as he knew, he had no enemies in the magical community.

He opened his eyes, but his vision remained dark and he realized there was no light source anywhere. His enhanced eyesight took some time to adjust, but eventually the room came into focus. Not that there was anything to see. He was sitting on a chair inside a storage room, piles of boxes and old furniture around him. When he tried to move his hands, he realized they were cuffed behind him, his feet cuffed to the chair's legs.

Despite the musty smell permeating the air, the trace of a scent hit his nose. It was familiar for some reason. Something briny. A Lycan had been in here, he was sure of it. But, except for the New York clan, he rarely had any contact with others of his kind.

He didn't know why a Lycan would kidnap him, but he had to get out of here. Whoever took him knew about Luna. Why else would they make him think they had her? And they also knew she was his True Mate. Were these the men who tried to kill her?

He took a deep breath, calling his inner wolf. Shifting into his Lycan form would be enough to break the metal cuffs. It would hurt like hell, but he'd heal.

The door suddenly opened and the sound of a gun cocking made him pause. "Uh-uh. I don't think so. Not unless you want me to pump you full of bullets while in mid-shift?"

Another Lycan. He smelled like mint. "I could try," he replied.

The Lycan laughed. "You could. But, you don't want us to kill your mate, do you?"

"I'm not falling for that one again."

"We really do have her this time. Your brothers and sister too." The Lycan walked into the room and pressed his gun to Killian's temple. "Get him out."

Two more men—no, Lycans too—walked behind him. The cuffs around his ankles came off, and then a pair of hands looped under his arms and hauled him out of the chair. Pain shot through his shoulder as he twisted his torso away trying to get away from them.

"Don't fuck with me!" The butt of a gun slammed against his forehead, and he saw stars. "We still have some of that confounding potion. I'll use it if I have to."

"Asshole," Killian muttered.

"Shut up."

The two Lycans hauled him away and he shut his eyes as the light assaulted his vision for a moment. His eyes adjusted as he let them drag him away. Dread pooled in his stomach. He had a very bad feeling about this.

His instinct was right. When the Lycans pushed him into the next room down the hallway, his eyes were immediately drawn to the four figures in the middle. Connor. Quinn. Meredith. Daric. They were all sitting in chairs, their hands behind them, probably cuffed as he had been. Killian frowned. The Lycan said he also had Luna.

"Finally awake," a voice said. "That confounding potion was a little strong, but that's to compensate for Lycan metabolism."

Killian slowly turned his head, the pool of dread growing. Luna was standing on the other side of the room and there was a figure behind her, pointing a gun at her head. Her violet eyes were wide, filled with fear and her breath came in short gasps.

When he made a move to come closer, the man pushed the muzzle against her temple. "Stay where you are, Killian." The man's face was in the shadow, but there was something about that voice that was familiar.

"Who the hell are you? And why did you bring me here? Did you kidnap my family and my mate, too?"

"No, they came here on their own, on some foolish mission to rescue you." The man walked closer, pushing Luna along.

Killian's blood froze in his veins. He knew that voice, as well as the scent of brine drifted into his nostrils.

"Is it coming back? You were so young, but surely you must remember me, boy." As he came to the light, the Lycan's mouth twisted into a mocking smile. He had dirty blonde hair cropped close to his scalp and an ugly nose, probably broken too many times. The Lycan was large, but still shorter than Killian, though he was built like a linebacker with wide shoulders and powerful arms.

"*You.*" Killian swallowed and sweat beaded at his temple. He tried to clamp down the memories that were flooding back into his mind. Blood and smoke. Being lifted up into beefy arms.

The smell of brine. And dirty sheets over a thin mattress in a single room. "You took me. You killed my clan."

He laughed. "That's right, boy."

Killian gritted his teeth. "Ray." That was his name. He heard one of the men call him that, which earned him a smack from Ray. They weren't supposed to use names. All these memories were coming back to him. The other children from his clan—all gone. "You killed my clan and kept us in that place. Then when I escaped, you killed the other kids."

"Almost correct." Ray's smile turned feral. "I did kill your entire clan. But when that man took you, I didn't have a choice. I took the kids with me and burned that facility to the ground."

"Why did you take us?"

Ray spat on the ground. "I was going to build up my training facility and have all you pups whipped into shape. A Lycan army, trained by the best from childhood." He huffed. "That yellow-bellied fool, Rodrigo Baeles. He was my partner in this little venture. But, he got nervous when you escaped and scrapped my plan."

"And the kids?"

"Why, who do you think's been helping me all this time, boy?"

Killian looked at him. The three Lycans who took him from the room. Probably more, guarding the facility. Ray had somehow twisted them up and turned them into his own personal Lycan army.

"What do you want, Ray?" he asked. "Why go to all this trouble to kidnap me?"

"Do you think what I did was going to stay under the radar for long? With the council unraveling Rodrigo's treachery, he was bound to name me and tell them what I did. I knew I had to silence the only other willing witness and victim. You." Ray laughed. "I've been keeping tabs on you, boy. And I know about this one," he pulled Luna by the arm, making her whimper in pain. "Your True Mate. She's got that pup of yours in her. I ran her over myself to make sure."

"Monster!" Luna cried.

Ray pushed her down on the floor to her knees. "Shut up, bitch!" He turned to Killian. "I was going to kidnap her to lure you here too. But those humans I hired were no match for you."

"You already have me," Killian said. "Let them go. You can do what you want with me."

"You think I'm going to let you all go? You're stupider than I thought. I can't do that. I'll have the Alpha of New York and the Creed Dragon on my ass." He tsked and looked at the others. "You shouldn't have followed him. Now I'm going to have to kill you all." He looked at Luna. "Starting with you."

"Bastard!" Killian's wolf was seething, wanting to be let out. But he couldn't risk it. Even if Luna and Meredith survived, he could still kill Connor, Daric, and Quinn.

"Hey, dickweed!" Meredith called. "You can't hurt her, remember? She's a pregnant True Mate. And so am I."

"Oh yeah?" Ray cocked his gun. "Do you think a True Mate could survive having her brains splattered all over the floor? At this range, her brain will turn to mush before it could heal itself." He laughed. "Of course, if she does survive, I'm sure I could find other ways to torture her."

"Fucking asshole! You touch her and I'll..." Killian lunged for Ray, but the two Lycans beside him grabbed his arm and pulled him to his knees.

Ray snickered. "I don't think so, boy. Don't even think about shifting!"

The muscles under Killian's skin began to move and ripple. The threat to Luna and the pup was agitating his inner wolf, and he struggled to break free.

"Control yourself! I don't have to kill her to hurt her!"

"Daric, now!"

Ray's eyes grew wide in shock as the gun disappeared from his hand. Seizing the opening, Killian let the wolf rip from his skin and lunged for Ray. Luna rolled to the side, shielding herself as the massive black wolf leaped over her. Ray himself was beginning to shift into wolf form, but Killian's teeth sank into his middle, slowing him down. The other Lycan let out a blood-curdling scream as claws and fangs ripped into his skin. Rivers of red ran down the wolf's jaw, but he kept going. Around him, snarls and howls of other wolves rang through the abandoned mansion. His family. They were protecting each other.

As Ray let out his last breaths, Killian backed away. The bastard was finally dead. Despite not knowing that Ray had been stalking him his whole life, Killian felt a sense of relief.

He turned, searching for his mate. Luna was huddled in a corner, tears streaming down her cheeks and clutching her stomach. The look of fear in her eyes was something he would never forget and only added to the guilt he felt. She wouldn't be here if it weren't for him.

"Killian!" Meredith called. "It's over."

He swung his head around. Two of the Lycans were down, naked in their human forms and clutching at their wounds. Quinn had a scrap of fabric over a bite on his shoulder to stop it from bleeding out, but the wound was nothing a few days of rest wouldn't heal. Connor was still in wolf form, his massive paws holding one of them down. The feral wolf was spitting and gnashing at his victim, and as he prepared to sink his teeth into his victim, Meredith stopped him.

"Stop! Connor! He's done!" She sprinted toward Connor, planting herself next to him.

The feral wolf roared in Meredith's face, but she remained still, back stiff and hands on her hips in a show of bravery. The animal let out a last growl and backed away, slowly retreating.

Killian turned back to Luna who was getting to her feet. He called his wolf, pushing it back until his inky black fur began to recede and his long limbs shortened.

"*Killian*," Luna whispered, her eyes roaming over his human body.

He waited for her to recoil, but was caught off guard when she launched herself into his arms. Her sweet scent filled his senses, and the tension left his body. His hand went immediately to her stomach, and he felt the flutter of movement there. Relief and happiness washed over him. Luna was alive and their child was safe.

"I don't...what happened?" she murmured against his chest.

"Ray didn't know Daric was a warlock," Meredith supplied.

"It took some time, but I was able to turn the metal into something more breakable while Ray was distracted," Daric added, nodding to where they had been bound to the chairs. Shards of glass lay on the floor. "And then it was simply a matter of transporting the gun from his hand and sending it somewhere else."

"Connor?" Killian asked as he looked around for his brother.

Quinn shrugged. "You know him. He needs some time to change back."

"Right." He looked down at Luna, who still clung to him. "Let's sort this out. Daric, can you conjure something up to restrain those other Lycans?"

"I'll see what I can do," the warlock answered.

"Quinn—contact Sebastian and Grant. They'll want to know what happened." His brother nodded and fished his phone out of his pocket.

As they walked out of the room, Killian shielded Luna's eyes from looking at Ray's dead body on the floor. No, she didn't have to see that. And if he had his way, she would never be caught in the crossfire like that again.

20

Grant Anderson sent his Beta, Nick Vrost to the scene. He arrived with other Lycans from the New York clan's security force, plus Sebastian Creed. Nick instructed his people to gather the Lycans who had been under Ray's control and take them back to the basement level of Fenrir's headquarters. The Beta also assured Killian that the clan would take care of Ray's body and that none of the Lone Wolves would have to worry about backlash from the High Council or any human authority.

Luna couldn't wait to get out of there. She was still shaking inside the car as they drove back to New York. The farther away she was from that place, the better. She cuddled next to Killian and he pulled her closer. She had nearly lost him today, making her realize just how much she loved him. Yet, try as she might, the words wouldn't come out of her mouth.

Sebastian dropped them off at Killian's place, Luna following along behind him as they walked into his apartment. Neither said a word as they entered and the tension was thick in the air as if each were afraid to speak. She was scared to break the silence. The lump in her throat that had built up during the ride back was still there, and she knew that if she spoke first, the dam would break and she wouldn't be able to handle all the emotions that were bubbling up inside of her. But then again, if she didn't say anything, she feared her heart would burst.

"I—"

Killian stopped her with his mouth, urgent and almost pleading. Luna sighed against him, melting into him and letting him carry her into the bedroom. He didn't turn the lights on as he laid her down. The only illumination in the room was the moon streaming through the windows and the lights of the city outside. He shucked off his jacket, shirt, and pants and lay beside her then began to slowly and reverently remove her clothes.

He made love to her with an unhurried pace. It wasn't like the last time when he was punishing himself by delaying his pleasure. However, it was even more intense, as if he was savoring her as if he would never make love to her again. When she cried out her orgasm, Killian wrapped his arms around her so tight as he found his release, she feared she would lose the air in her lungs. As they lay there quietly, he pulled her to him, whispering something unintelligible in her ear. She wasn't sure what it was, but sleep claimed her exhausted body. As she drifted off, she resolved that they were going to have a long talk, but it would have to wait until morning.

The sun wasn't even up yet when Luna awoke. The room was still dark, and the clock beside her said it was just after four. She glanced around at the empty bed. Killian's scent lingered on the pillows, but he was nowhere in sight.

Slipping on a new nightgown from the closet, she walked out to the living room to look for him. He was there, sitting on the couch with his face in his hands.

"Killian," she called, her voice still raspy from sleep. "What are you doing? Come back to bed."

He looked up at her, but didn't say anything. With a sigh, she padded over to the couch. "Something's wrong. Tell me, what's going on." She sat down beside him.

"I put you in danger," he said in a hoarse voice. "You and our baby. You could have died today. Or worse. I thought someone from your past was out to get you, but I was wrong. It was *my* past coming back to haunt *me*."

"Killian," she began. "Don't, please."

"No—it's all my fault! Even Bakersfield was my fault. He thought you were in on the theft." He stood up and grabbed a piece of paper from the coffee table. "I won't have you or our child in danger anymore." He walked over to the window, gazing over the city.

"We won't be." She stood up and walked over to him. "You're going to protect us from now on."

"Yes." He pivoted to face her. "And here's how," he said as he handed her the paper in his hands.

"What is it?" Her eyes scanned over the sheet. Deed...Luna Rhoades...her old address in Portland. "Killian?"

"I bought it for you and the baby," he answered quickly. "So you can be safe and away from danger. The press has already picked up the Bakersfield story, and I'm sure it won't take long for the Portland Museum of Art to offer you your old job back."

Luna stood there silently, but inside, her heart was breaking into a million pieces. "What about the baby?"

"You can have full custody. We can work out an agreement and I can fly over every weekend. Or we can have lawyers deal with it. Your choice."

Emotions swirled through her and she turned to walk away. She was halfway down the hallway when she stopped. Whirling around, she walked back into the living room where he remained rooted to the spot near the window, gazing outside.

"Killian," she called in a determined voice.

"I'll give you whatever support you need." He didn't even turn to face her. "Whatever you want. Clothes, food, private schools, tutoring, sports—whatever it is the kid needs."

Anger suddenly boiled in her. "The kid?" she asked, her voice pitching higher. "That's how you're going to refer to our child now?"

"What else do you want, Luna?" He pivoted to her, his eyes hard as steel. "I'm doing my best to protect you."

"Protect me?" She stomped to him, her hands on her hips. "How can you protect me when you're halfway across the country?"

"That is how I'm protecting you both!" He put his hands up.

"By sending me away?" Tears began to form in her eyes, but she refused to turn away. She wanted him to see how much he was hurting her. "You want me to leave?"

"Christ, no! But I'm not forcing you to live with me. Not when I took everything away from you. I love you too damn much to watch you wither away and slowly hate me for the rest of your life. That's why I'm giving you this chance to have your old life back."

Luna stood very still. She thought he was still saying something, but her ears were buzzing. Killian loved her? Killian loved her!

"You love me?" she asked, interrupting him.

"Yes," he admitted, his hands falling to his sides.

"Then why are you pushing me away?" Her mind was still reeling.

"Haven't you been listening to what I've been saying?"

Killian grabbed her arms. "I know everything. What happened to you after I left. And your father—"

"My father has nothing to do with this!" she exclaimed. "*Killian, please*. Don't do this. I love you too and I want to be with you." The tears were now falling down her cheeks, and she couldn't stop them. He let go of her, his face in complete shock. "Please," she begged, holding on to his arms. "Don't send me away. I want to be with you. I want to live here with you and buy you more furniture and have our baby in New York. I want us to raise this baby together and then give him or her more brothers and sisters—"

His mouth on hers stopped her babbling, and she let out a sob against his lips. Strong arms encircled her and drew her close.

"Luna," he whispered against her lips. "I don't deserve you."

She put a finger on his mouth. "Shush. I won't have you talking like that."

"It's true," he sighed. "But I'm going to damn well make sure that someday, I'll be good enough for you."

"You are good enough for me." She gave him a peck on the nose. "You're loyal, kind, gentle, and forgiving."

"But still I took everything away from you. Your life—"

"My old life," she corrected. "Now I have a new one." She took his hand and placed it over her belly then put her palm on top. "You may think you took everything away from me, Killian, but you gave me the most precious thing in the world."

"Our baby."

"Yes," she replied. "And your heart."

Killian kneeled down and laid his head on her stomach. "I love you, Luna. And I love you, baby." He gave her belly a kiss. "I promise, I'm going to be the best dad ever. I'm going to love you and protect you both. Forever."

Tears sprang from Luna's eyes again, but this time, they were for a different reason. "That's all I ever wanted."

21

"Well, this is an unusual stop for a babymoon," Luna said as she stared up at the Neoclassical Revival-style building. The facade of the structure was undergoing a facelift and half of the front was covered in scaffolding. The din of hammering and drilling filled the air around them as the construction workers labored to get the National Museum of Mornavia ready for its grand re-opening next week.

Killian came up from behind, wrapped his arms around her and laid his hands on her well-rounded belly. "Well, this trip was about taking you to see all the great artworks in the world before the baby came."

Her lips curved into a naughty smile. "Amongst other things."

The last two months had been the happiest in Killian's life. Sure, he had to make some adjustments living with Luna, but he was glad to put the ugliness of the past behind them. Coming home to her was the best part of his day, and he'd let her decorate his apartment to her heart's content. She'd kept the same furniture, but added a few of her own touches here and there.

The nursery in particular was her pride and joy, and she spent a lot of time making it perfect for their baby.

She'd kept the apartment in Portland, but only because he had bought it for her and together had decided it would make a nice getaway. With Luna's mom and the Van der Meers still in Oregon, they would be making frequent visits to the city anyway. Her family were quite surprised when she announced her pregnancy and initially suspicious of Killian, but it was quickly replaced with acceptance and joy when they saw how happy she was with him.

He had been eager to take her away on a 'babymoon' before the birth of their child, but he couldn't go right away because of work. Plus, he felt some obligation towards the Lycans who had been under Ray's control. Currently, there were five who were detained by the New York Clan. They should have been sent to the Lycan prison facility in Siberia, but he wanted to help rehabilitate them if it were at all possible. After all, they were all trapped by the same circumstances, and he had been the lucky one that got away. While the Lycans were angry at being kept prisoner, none of them seemed to show any loyalty to Ray and Killian had hope for them.

So after two months, he finally got some time off, and he took Luna on a trip to Rome, Florence, Paris, London, and Madrid. He remembered her favorite artworks and they went to see them all. And now they were on their last stop, one that he'd saved for last and kept as a surprise.

He took her hand and led her to the entrance of the museum, careful to avoid the tools and equipment scattered around.

"Killian, they're not open yet," Luna warned. "Should we be up here?"

He said nothing, but smiled at her as he opened the door and led them in.

"Ah, Mr. Killian." An older Mornavian man was waiting by the lobby desk, his smile wide. "We've been expecting you. I'm Adam Dalko, Director of the National Museum of Mornavia."

"Please, call me Killian," he said, extending his hand. The older man took it heartily and shook it.

"Luna Rhoades." She offered her hand to Dalko. "*Drago mi je*," she said, hoping her pronunciation of the Mornavian words was correct.

"Ah, smart as you are lovely," Dalko said. "Well, he's waiting for you. Please, come this way."

Her brows furrowed, but Killian remained silent as they followed Dalko to the main hall. They went up a flight of stairs, and then down a hallway and into a large room.

There was a figure standing next to a display case covered with a white sheet. His back was to them, but as they approached, he turned to face them. Luna's jaw dropped when she saw his face.

"Killian," Bogdan Martinov, the president of Mornavia greeted him. "Lovely to see you again, I'm glad you made it. And this must be your Luna." He smiled warmly at them, the wrinkles on his face deepening.

"Your Excellency," Killian nodded. "Thank you for giving us this opportunity."

"Uh...nice to meet you, Your Excellency." Luna stuttered. "Killian, what's going on?" she whispered.

"I'm happy you finally came back, Killian," Martinov continued. "So you can see the result of your work for us." He nodded to Dalko, who was standing next to the display case. The director tugged on the sheet.

Luna let out a gasp. "It's the..."

"Yes, the *Gastlava Tapestry*—she is finally home." Martinov's eyes were misty as he looked up at the tapestry behind the display case. "Thanks to your work, we will finally be able to unveil her for our people and the world to see."

"And the press?"

Martinov nodded. "They will be told that an anonymous donor delivered the tapestry to the museum. And with Bakersfield's legal troubles, I'm sure he'll be too busy to try and take it from us."

"Don't worry. If he does, I'll convince him that it won't be worth his while," Killian added.

"On behalf of the people of Mornavia, we give you our deepest thanks. And because you waived your usual fee, we were able to put the money to good use to restore the museum." He nodded at Dalko. "We will give you a few minutes alone so you can enjoy the tapestry." With that, the two men left.

Luna looked up at him, her violet eyes wide with shock. "All this time, Killian? You didn't tell me you stole it to give it back to Mornavia."

He shrugged. "Would it have made a difference? I still ruined—"

"*Shhh.*' She put a finger to his lips. "I told you never to say that again. It upsets me. And the baby." She took his hand and put it on her stomach. He felt a strong kick against his palm, which made him smile. "I suppose I wouldn't have hated you so much back then. I really thought you were doing it for the money."

"I was," he confessed. "But, the way you talked about the tapestry and how art should be enjoyed by everyone...well...I couldn't take their money. Anyway, the President arranged this viewing just for us. You should enjoy it."

She flashed him a smile and stepped forward to peer at the tapestry. "It's so beautiful. I couldn't get up close because they had all this security around it." She pressed her nose to the glass. "The detailing is magnificent."

Killian swallowed a gulp, his hands suddenly sweaty. *Now or never*, he thought as he got down on one knee and took out the box from his pocket.

"And these colors! Where could the weaver have found such hues in that time? Oh, this must have looked even better when —" She stopped dead when she turned around and put her hand over her mouth. Her eyes dropped to the magnificent diamond ring nestled in black velvet.

"Luna, I love you, and I want to be with you forever. Will you marry me, please?"

"I...I...of course I'll marry you!" Luna exclaimed.

He slipped the diamond ring on her finger and stood up, then pulled her into his arms for a long, passionate kiss.

"I don't want to wait too long," he said as he pulled away. "But I'll understand if you want to wait until after the baby's born and have a big wedding. Whatever you want, sweetheart."

She shook her head. "No, I don't want to wait either."

"Good. How do you feel about a Vegas ceremony?"

EPILOGUE

$\mathcal{I}$t took about twenty-four hours to arrange their quickie ceremony in Vegas. They went back to their hotel and called everyone they wanted to come and arranged for their flights.

"Vegas—really?" Meredith said over video chat from the the lobby of Lone Wolf Security. "Is Elvis going to officiate?"

"I thought you'd like Vegas," Luna said. "It's a fun town."

"Yeah, but that means your choices are limited if you want me there." She paused. "I'm banned at The Mirage and Caesar's Palace. Also, forget Excalibur, Luxor, Paris, and the Palms. Hey Quinn!" she called out.

"What?" Quinn's voice answered from off screen.

"That job with the Python and the 10 gallons of jello—was that MGM or Bellagio?"

"That was MGM. Bellagio was the hornet's nest and the Furry convention."

"Right." She turned back to the screen. "So, anywhere except those places."

"And The Palazzo!" Quinn added. "Though I maintain to this day that I wasn't using a card-counting machine."

"No worries then. It's just a quickie ceremony at the Chapel of Love on the strip," Luna replied. Her definition of normal had definitely changed. "Just make sure you get everyone there on time, okay?"

"Aye, aye, captain." Meredith gave her a salute before hanging up.

In the end, everyone they wanted to witness their ceremony was there. The Van der Meers, Luna's mom Julia, Connor, Quinn, Meredith, Daric, Jade, and Sebastian were already in Vegas by the time they arrived. Grant and Frankie gave their apologies for missing the wedding as their twins, Adrianna and Lucas, were just turning a month old and the new parents couldn't bear the thought of leaving their precious ones behind.

Luna found a white dress she liked (wedding maternity dresses were ridiculously easy to find in Vegas) and Killian picked the first suit off the rack at the shopping mall near their hotel. Meredith and Connor were maid of honor and best man. An Elvis impersonator did *not* marry the happy couple.

Since their choices of wedding reception places were limited in Vegas, they all decided to fly home to New York. Much to Luna's amusement, Killian had reserved a banquet hall in Chinatown for their reception with Emerald Dragon catering the entire affair. Mrs. Tan was waiting for them in front of the building, dressed in a beautiful purple *qipao*. She had a knowing grin on her face as she welcomed the happy couple.

They sat on the dais at the front of the banquet hall, enjoying the feast of lobster, chicken, scallops, and a wide variety of dishes, surrounded by their family and friends. Behind them, there was a red and gold cutout of a Chinese character which Mrs. Tan had explained meant, 'double happiness', a traditional symbol of marriage. The older woman had also arranged for a lion dance for their reception, and everyone enjoyed how the skillful acrobats managed the leaps and jumps from the narrow platforms set up in the middle of the dance floor.

"Are you happy with our wedding, sweetheart?" he asked as he wrapped an arm around her waist. "Did you wish we waited?"

"Are you kidding?" she asked, her eyes never leaving the lion dancers. "This is the best wedding ever. And I wasn't going to wait for another second to marry you."

He kissed her temple. "Good." His hand moved over her belly and, as if agreeing with Luna, the baby gave him a good kick. "Hope that one wasn't too bad. Maybe he'll be a pro footballer."

"Or a Rockette," she replied in an amused voice.

"Sweetheart, our baby can be whoever he or she wants."

She tipped her head back and he kissed her on the lips. In the corner of her eyes, the gold and red paper seemed to shimmer. Double happiness, indeed.

EXTENDED EPILOGUE

Five years later...

"Luna! Killian! I'm coming in, ready or not," Meredith shouted through the door.

Luna let out a sigh and looked at her husband, who was currently trying to coax their youngest, three-year-old Olivia, into her dress.

"I don't wanna go, daddy," she pouted, and crossed her chubby arms. She was still wearing her pajamas.

"Please, pumpkin?" Killian waved the pink dress in front of the girl. "C'mon, Auntie Meredith is here."

"Auntie Meredith is here! Auntie Meredith is here!" Arch, their eldest, came zooming down the hallway. He was already dressed in his jeans and shirt but was still barefoot. As Meredith came through the door, he launched himself into her arms, nearly sending his aunt to the ground.

"Arch!" Luna said, putting her hands on her waist. "You

know you can't roughhouse with Auntie Meredith when she has a baby in her tummy."

"Sorry, Auntie Mer," Arch said, bowing his head.

"It's all right, kiddo," Meredith ruffled his hair. "Me and the baby are all right. We're pretty tough, you know. He or she is protecting me like you did when you were in your mommy's tummy." She rubbed her belly. "Hey, is Olivia ready too?"

"Kinda," he nodded to Killian and Olivia. The little girl was still pouting and Killian was beginning to lose his patience.

"Awww, c'mere baby." Meredith walked over to the father and daughter, opening her arms. Olivia immediately ran to her aunt then broke out into a fierce sob.

"Daddy's being mean!" she cried. "I said I don't wanna go. I wanna stay here with him and mommy!"

"You don't want to come with me and Uncle Daric and your cousins? They're waiting downstairs for you," Meredith said, patting the little girl's back. "And you know everyone's going to be at the barbecue. Arch is coming and Lucas, Adrianna, Julianna, Mika, Dee, Nathan…all your friends will be there, too."

Violet eyes peered up at her as if trying to judge if she was lying or not. "Well…I guess it's okay. We'll come back after, right?"

"I promise, we'll drop you back here—unless you want to have a sleepover at my house? I bet I could ask Uncle Daric to show you some cool tricks he's been working on."

"Really? Yay!" The little girl kissed Meredith and grabbed the dress from her father's hands. She ran to her room, whipping off her pajamas on the way, and was naked by the time she disappeared through the door into her room.

Killian gave Meredith a grateful nod. "Thanks."

His sister sighed. "If only I could get my boys to do as I say. I heard girls are much easier."

"Think it'll be a girl this time?" Luna asked, looking at Meredith's belly.

"I freaking hope so," she answered. "But don't tell Daric that. I think he secretly loves that I'm outnumbered at home."

Luna laughed. "At least you're not deadlocked in a tie all the time. It's always boys versus girls around here."

"Maybe we'll make our little tie-breaker today, huh?" Killian said, giving her ass a squeeze.

"You better," Meredith retorted. "I'm not driving into Long Island with four toddlers for nothing! At least maybe you'll get lucky," she winked at Luna.

"She got lucky last night," Killian informed her. "But, we had to cut naked cuddling time short when Olivia had a nightmare and crawled into our bed."

"You and mommy cuddle naked?" Arch asked as he popped his head from behind Luna. "That's gross!" His little nose wrinkled.

Meredith laughed. "Aww, kiddo. If mommy and daddy didn't cuddle naked, you wouldn't be here right now."

The little boy looked confused. "What does that mean?" He looked up to his father. "Daddy, what's Auntie Meredith saying?"

Killian shot his sister a glare. "Go ask her. No, wait, don't do that. I promise I'll tell you when you get back, okay?" He picked up his son and gave him a kiss on the cheek then handed him to Luna so she could kiss him goodbye.

"I'm ready, I'm ready, woohoo!" Olivia screamed as she ran back into the room, wearing the pink dress. "Let's go, Auntie Mer!"

"Okay kiddos, go grab your things." As the two children grabbed their backpacks, Meredith turned to Luna and Killian. "Are you sure you guys don't want to come along? You know

Grant and Frankie always have a fabulous spread at these things."

Luna gave her a smirk and looked at Killian. "Naw, we're fine here."

"Naked cuddle time. Right."

"Thanks for offering to take the kids," he said. "Be good," he warned the two toddlers.

"Yes, daddy!" they said in unison.

"See you guys!" Meredith ushered Arch and Olivia out the door.

"Finally," he said with a relieved sigh. "I have you alone."

Luna giggled as her husband swept her up and carried her bridal-style to their bedroom. She didn't think it was possible, but each year they were together, she only became happier and more in love with Killian. Sure, there were ups and downs, but she wouldn't have wanted her life to turn out any other way. After she had given birth to Arch, she went back to work part-time at the Tisch Gallery. She realized that she loved mentoring and tutoring students and up-and-coming artists, so she got a job at the New York University's Fine Arts Department. She worked part-time, and with the flexible hours, she could still spend time at home with the kids.

Killian, too, had made a few changes at work. Lone Wolf Security was thriving under his leadership, and they had added a few more Lycans to their roster. In fact, three of the Lycans from Ray's gang became their most loyal and trusted employees. With the additional staff, he didn't have to go overseas as much (or file paperwork, which he thought was the best part.)

"Ohhh, baby," Luna moaned when Killian's fingers skimmed over her panties. She looked down at his hand between her legs, her eyes glancing at the wolf's head tattoo on his forearm. Killian had told her what it meant, and although he wasn't a Lone Wolf anymore, (after having pledged to New York), it would always be there as a reminder of his past. And that was one of the things she loved most about him. Although he kept his eyes on the future, Killian never forgot where he came from and how hard he fought to get to where they were now.

"Slow down," she giggled when he yanked down her panties. "We have all day."

"Sweetheart," he grinned as he positioned himself between her legs. "We have the rest of our lives."

THANKS FOR READING!

But before you go, do want to read (**hot, sexy and explicit**) bonus scenes from this book, featuring Luna and Killian's first date and the day after? Join my Reading Group now! You'll get access to my super secret goodies page on my website where you can download these bonus scenes and some free e-novels.
Go to
http://aliciamontgomeryauthor.com/mailing-list/

I love hearing from readers and if you want to tell me what you think do let me know at alicia@aliciamontgomeryauthor.com

Connect with Alicia Montgomery:
http://aliciamontgomeryauthor.com/
https://www.facebook.com/aliciamontgomeryauthor/
https://twitter.com/amontromance

ABOUT THE AUTHOR

Alicia Montgomery has always dreamed of becoming a romance novel writer. She started writing down her stories in now long-forgotten diaries and notebooks, never thinking that her dream would come true. After taking the well-worn path to a stable career, she is now plunging into the world of self-publishing.

Sexy shifters, billionaires, alpha males, and of course, strong, sexy female characters are her favorite to write. Alicia is a wanderer, along with her husband, they travel the world and have lived in various spots all over the world.

AUTHOR'S NOTES

June 21, 2017

I'm writing this approximately two weeks after my wedding anniversary. While JT and I had a very different wedding from Killian and Luna, I couldn't help but sprinkle in a few elements from our own reception. Having lived in China for a bit (and my own great-Grandmother being of Chinese descent), we had to have the double happiness symbol in our wedding. The same characters we had still hangs outside our bedroom door to this day, and we plan to take it with us to our next destination (wherever and whenever that may be).

I thought that Tempted by the Wolf would be the end, but really, it was just the beginning. Writing this series has been so immensely satisfying. Frustrating sometimes, especially when certain characters refused to talk to me (I'm looking at you, Daric), but typing out every single word has been a joy. I really hope you liked the beginning of the Lone Wolf Defender series. By the time I was outlining Tempting by the Wolf, I really thought I would be done with the world of the New York Lycans. I was ready to move on. But, when I started writing about Killian, Quinn, and Connor, I knew that they had to have their own stories, too.

I can't wait to bring you Quinn's story. It's going to be a much different tone, and from the way he's been knocking around in my head, I can tell it's going to be a fun one to write. And some of you have already told me they are dying for Connor's story. He'll be here soon, don't worry.

I love hearing from you guys, so please do drop me a line at alicia@aliciamontgomeryauthor.com and tell me what you think. If you loved Killian's Secret and all the other books in the True Mates Series, thank you so much (and I hope maybe you leave me a review). And if you don't like the book, and want to tell me why, I welcome those types of emails too. It helps me a lot as a writer, so I can get to know my audience and what they like and don't like.

I'll stop babbling and start writing (I hear you, Quinn!).

All the best,

Alicia

Printed in Great Britain
by Amazon